THE GOLD MINE AT PUEBLO PEQUEÑO

In Del Rio, Johnny Dark, persuaded by stranger Nathan King, joins him in a deadly race to regain ownership of a gold mine. But nothing turns out the way King predicted. Five years later, to discover the truth behind certain tragic events, Dark rides to Del Rio with his wife, Cath. But he's immediately drawn into a gun battle against outlaws and the gold mine at Pueblo Pequeño — and the outcome is doubtful until the final shot is fired.

WILL KEEN

THE GOLD MINE AT PUEBLO PEQUEÑO

Complete and Unabridged

LINFORD
Leicester

First published in Great Britain in 2007 by
Robert Hale Limited
London

First Linford Edition
published 2008
by arrangement with
Robert Hale Limited
London

British Library CIP Data

Keen, Will, *1936–*
The gold mine at Pueblo Pequeño.—
Large print ed.—
Linford western library
1. Western stories
2. Large type books
I. Title
823.9'14 [F]

ISBN 978–1–84782–282–6

Published by
F. A. Thorpe (Publishing)
Anstey, Leicestershire

Set by Words & Graphics Ltd.
Anstey, Leicestershire
Printed and bound in Great Britain by
T. J. International Ltd., Padstow, Cornwall

This book is printed on acid-free paper

PART ONE

1

1890

Their gaze alighted on him as he slapped open the saloon's doors, caught the hard rebound with his forearm and stepped through. They were sitting at a table in the centre of the room. On the table there was a pack of playing cards, and a bottle of whiskey. No glasses. It was the fat one's turn to drink. He was a black-eyed Mex with greasy hair under a big, shabby sombrero glittering with silver conchos. The scar slicing through the stubble on his jaw turned white as he tilted the bottle and took a long pull. The other man, leaning back in his chair with long legs spread, was a lean drifter with hair like dry straw brushing his filthy collar. His eyes were cold enough to freeze axle grease.

Trouble, Johnny Dark sensed. And,

as always, he felt his heartbeat quicken, felt his senses sing to the sudden excitement that raced through him like a prairie fire running wild. Excitement — and resentment. Why, he thought? Why in God's name did it always come down to this?

Shadows were long. Late afternoon sunlight was slanting across Del Rio's shabby false fronts and through the saloon's dusty windows. Motes like fine gold dust drifted lazily in the shafts of dazzling light, then swirled as if caught in a sudden breeze as Dark strode lithely to the bar.

He ordered his drink. Accepted the glass with a grunt of thanks and with a twist of his fingers set a coin spinning musically on the warped boards. Then he turned and, glass in hand, deliberately reined in his excitement and let his wryly amused gaze wander around the room.

It was the time of day before work finished, so the place was quiet. The thin man in ragged clothing hanging on

4

to the end of the long bar had probably been there since the doors opened, and would be kicked into the dusty street just before they closed. The local drunk, Dark figured. One in every town. Then, over near the window, a man somewhere between middle and old age had his elbows on the table and appeared to be staring moodily into a glass of pale beer while one hand absently stroked a drooping dragoon moustache. A flat-crowned black hat with a plaited rawhide band was tipped forward, hiding his eyes. Dark wasn't fooled. A watcher, he figured. He won't miss a trick.

That left the two gunslingers.

They were still taking turns with the bottle. And they were watching Dark.

Dark let his gaze settle when it reached them. He stared insolently at the gaunt character with eyes like chips of ice, lifted his glass, took a drink of the fiery liquid. Then, as if dismissing what he was seeing as of no consequence, he deliberately shook his head and turned back to the bar.

There was a faint clink as the slick-haired man behind the bar put down the glass he'd been polishing. He flicked the grubby cloth over one shoulder, planted his hands on the bar.

'You tired of living?'

'Why?' Dark said, and looked with concern at his empty glass. 'You servin' poisoned whiskey?'

The dark haired saloonist's eyes were sardonic.

'What are you? Eighteen? Nineteen?'

'That's not bad,' Dark said, 'for a wild guess.'

'Skinny, too. Soaking wet I'd say you're a whisker shy of a hundred and forty pounds.'

'If I include the gunbelt.'

'You'd better,' the saloonist said, 'because, son, you're going to need it.'

'What's that mean? Is the hobo using the bar as a crutch going to breathe on me? That old man over there bore me to death with camp-fire tales . . . '

His words died away as he watched

6

the light change in the saloonist's eyes. The absence of noise in the room had been restful. Now it was an uncomfortable silence throbbing with menace. Then, in that silence, he heard the whisper of unhurried footsteps.

Dark said, 'Give me another drink.'

The saloonist picked up the bottle and made as if to pour, but Dark stopped him.

'No. Leave it with me.'

For a moment the saloonist hesitated. His eyes looked beyond Dark, then flicked away nervously. He shrugged, placed the almost full whiskey bottle beside Dark's glass. As if glad to get away, he made it his business to serve the man at the far the end of the bar.

Dark took hold of the bottle. He held the neck with his left hand. The hand was twisted awkwardly, palm out, thumb and forefinger low down on the neck. Then he began to turn to his left, away from the bar. He moved his feet, but kept the bottom of the bottle firmly planted on the bar's board surface. It was almost impossible to turn his upper body — yet still he forced the turn. The effect of twisting against immoveable shoulders and arms was to tighten his muscles. Those tight muscles acquired the tension of a coiled steel spring. When Dark could turn no more without taking the bottle with him, he became still. Only his head moved. His head, and his eyes. Carefully controlling the trembling in his muscles caused by the fierce tension he had created, he glanced behind him.

Two paces behind Dark, the big Mexican's lips were parted in a wet grin. His hands were clenched into fists. His unshaven face was slick with sweat and his black eyes held an evil glint. Then they widened. Maybe he saw something he hadn't expected in Dark's eyes. He took a hasty half step backwards and dropped a meaty hand to the butt of his six-gun.

Instantly, Dark released the tension within his body. The hand holding the bottle came off the bar. He whipped it sideways. His body spun ahead of his arm. That arm was a flail, pulled in a vicious backhand swing by Dark's taut muscles. At the end of the flail the heavy bottle was a glistening blur.

The bottle hit the Mexican just above his left ear. There was a solid, sickening thud as of a cleaver biting into meat. The bottle shattered. Glass and whiskey sprayed across the room, sparkling in the shafts of sunlight. The sombrero flew from the Mexican's head. His eyes rolled so that only the whites showed as he toppled sideways. Then his knees buckled. He hit the sawdust with a thump, flopped onto his back and lay still. The big sombrero floated down and, like a wagon wheel, rolled towards the gaunt gunslinger.

He stood up. He came to his feet in one fluid movement and stepped quickly away from the table. A booted foot swung, kicked the sombrero out of his way. He turned away and made for the doors. He was walking without haste. As he stepped through the doors and into the full force of the evening sun, Dark saw him reach down and ease the six-gun in its oiled leather holster.

Then he paused, and looked back over his shoulder.

Dark nodded. He tossed the broken neck of the whiskey bottle onto the Mexican's fat belly, and followed the gaunt gunslinger out of the saloon.

2

'Why?' Dark said.

He was standing spread-legged in the dust of the street. The lean gunslinger was facing him some thirty feet away. He was squinting into the sinking sun. His right hand hovered like a claw above the butt of his six-gun.

In front of the business premises with their false fronts stripped clean of paint by the weather, the plank walks were empty. Three horses dozed at the saloon's hitch rail. Somewhere out back a dog barked. Then there was the creak of dry metal as the man with the black hat eased his way out of the saloon and let the doors clatter shut. He stepped to one side and leaned back lazily against the wall. Beneath the tipped brim of his hat his eyes were in shadow.

'What's that mean?' the lean drifter said, in a dry, rasping voice. 'What's this

11

'why' you're talking about? Is it why am I going to kill you? Or why don't I let you walk away? Or is it why — ?'

'What it is,' Dark said, 'is why do men like you take one look at me and get itchy, get overcome by the urge to use their fists, to knock me to the ground and stomp on me, to look at me along the barrel of a six-gun and murder — '

'Not murder. Hell, you're just a kid, I'll let you pull first — '

'But in your mind you know you're the faster gun so you know how it ends — I pull first, but I die. And if you know that, but still go ahead — isn't that murder?'

'Until we both pull iron there's no way of knowing.'

'What? You mean you're testing yourself? Using me, a skinny kid, as some measure of your skill, a reassurance that'll last only until the next one comes along?'

'Smart talk, but you're talking for the sake of it, talking to save your skin, playing for time so's — '

'Why?'

Like a bad toothache, the question wouldn't go away. Dark wouldn't let it. He watched the lean man, saw the realization in his eyes. And he waited, with a feeling of intense interest, for the answer.

'You're old enough to shave,' the gunslinger said, 'so you must know.'

Dark frowned. 'Make your point.'

'You get up in the morning, you shave. When you shave, you use a piece of glass, a cracked mirror. Every morning you look into that glass, you see the answer to your question.'

Again Dark frowned.

'When I look in the mirror, all I see is a skinny kid.'

'Yeah,' the lean man said, 'that's what I see, too, a skinny kid *with that goddamn air about him and that look in his eyes . . .* '

He flapped a hand impatiently. 'The talkin's all done — now make your play.'

Dark shook his head. 'If you're going to kill me, go ahead.'

'You ain't been listenin' — '

'I just changed the rules. The code. Whatever you call it. I'm sick of listening to men with hard voices making empty threats, sick of watching tired old men like you pull their six-guns like they're caught in a barrel of treacle, weary — '

The lean gunslinger's patience snapped. His body was still. The blazing eyes were turned a searing yellow by the light of the sun. They were fixed on Dark. Then his right hand moved. It flicked down to the holster. The clawed fingers clamped around the six-gun's butt. Light flashed as he drew the pistol. It came up in a blur. Cold steel glinted in the sun's rays. As the barrel came level the hammer snicked back.

The black hole of the muzzle threatened to swallow Dark. He watched a forefinger tighten on a trigger, caught himself marvelling at the way a complex series of movements had been executed

14

in less time than it takes for an eye to blink . . .

Then, as the forefinger applied pressure to release the cocked hammer, Johnny Dark moved.

Lazily, without haste, he made a draw that was too fast to see and shot the lean gunslinger through the right forearm. The sharp crack of the shot sent a black bird flapping and screeching from the saloon's roof. The man's levelled six-gun flew from suddenly nerveless fingers. It spun high, fell uselessly at his feet.

The lean man grabbed his arm. Blood trickled through his fingers, spattering the dust with dark spots.

'So now you know,' Dark said.

The gaunt man stared. His eyes were bright with pain, his teeth bared in a soundless snarl.

'You're fast,' he said hoarsely. 'But what you did was pure luck. You went for a centre shot — and missed.'

'Care to try again?'

'Another time, another place but,

sure, you've got it coming.'

'And next time from behind, so I don't get lucky?'

The lean man's mouth clamped shut. He bent and scooped up his pistol with his left hand, reached across his body to pouch it awkwardly, then turned his back on Dark and set off across the street.

Two blocks away, a door slammed. A man stepped down into the dust, slapping on his hat and hitching his gunbelt. On his vest a badge glittered.

From outside the saloon, the man in the black hat said his first words. He'd lifted his head. His eyes were as grey as winter, as shiny as river-wet stones.

'When you've finished with the law,' he said, in a voice as old as history, 'come and talk to me. I'll buy you a drink or two, and tell you how you can turn that skill into unimaginable riches.'

★　★　★

The keen-eyed marshal listened to Dark's story, spat, warned him not to look on the town as a place to settle down then wandered across the street to the rooming-house to talk to the bloodied gunslinger.

When Dark walked back into the saloon the big Mexican had gone, leaving behind a patch of dark blood in the dry sawdust. Two men, their blood spilled, but not a scratch on Dark. He smiled grimly. Maybe there was something in what had been said about a certain look. Maybe the men who noticed it should pay more heed to those warning signs of trouble. And that being so, Dark wondered, why was the old-timer interested, rather than repelled?

He found him at the same table near the window. The black hat had been removed, revealing thinning grey hair. Clearly he had been watching the street and had seen Dark's approach, for already there were two glasses on the table and a pitcher of cool beer.

'Nathan King,' he said, as Dark sat down, and he stuck out a hand like gnarled wood.

'Johnny Dark.'

'Uncannily fitting, from what I've observed.' King splashed beer into the glasses. 'Tell me, does a child get bestowed with a name that suits him from the outset? Or does he take what's given and pull it around him like a cloak in his formative years?'

'Either way,' Dark said, 'it didn't work for you.'

King chuckled. 'Royalty might not be the first thing crossing your mind when you look at me, but being a rich man might change the colour of your opinion.'

'So why don't you tell me about this unimaginable wealth?' Dark said, and he took a deep swallow of beer.

'As a start in that direction, I'd like to say I've got a map with a cross on it marking the site of a fabulous lost gold mine,' King said. He shook his head. 'But I haven't.'

'If you'd said that,' Dark said, 'I'd have thanked you for the beer and walked out the door.'

18

'Sure you would — '

King broke off. The slick-haired saloonist had come from behind the bar and was dragging his grubby rag across a nearby table. His lips were pursed in a soundless whistle as he ostentatiously averted his gaze. He heard the sudden silence, flashed a glance at King and quickly moved away.

'Sure you would,' King repeated, more quietly, 'so instead I'd like to tell you I know the exact location of the mine, and the papers proving owner-ship, in my name, are in my saddle-bags — but that would be only half right, and you want the whole truth.'

'Which half would be right?'

'I do know where the mine's located — but the papers, which are indeed in my name, were stolen.'

'Nice meeting you, Mr King.'

Dark drained his glass and pushed back his chair.

The gnarled hand clamped on his arm.

'Don't throw away a golden future

with one impulsive mistake.'

'You were watching, out there,' Dark said. 'What you witnessed should tell you I don't make mistakes.'

He shook off the restraining hand.

Nathan King said. 'Sit down. Please.'

The tone was soft, but underlying it there was an edge like a razor. The eyes were unchanged — or so Dark thought until he looked closer and saw in their dark depths a fire blazing. But what should he make of that? Was he seeing anger — or an unquenchable fervour? If fervour, where lay the cause?

He sat down.

Nathan King said, 'The man who stole those papers did it in a way that made the theft look legal. He cheated at cards. And he was good. Not a man at the table spotted what he was doing.'

'But you did?'

'It was *my* future that was at stake, *my* fortune hanging on the turn of a card.'

'If you knew he was cheating, why risk everything?'

'He'd already cleaned me out, taken every cent.'

'But all you did was delay the inevitable. In the end, by sleight of hand, a gambler took your mine and left you with nothing — right?'

'That's about the size of it.'

'If you were too late then, you're way too late now. He's got his hands on those papers.'

'Yes, but all he got from the papers he stole is the name of a mine. It wasn't a map; the mine's location is still a mystery. That means I'm still ahead of him. And you said it yourself, he's a gambler. A man like that lives easy, has soft white hands, and knows nothing about scraping gold out of raw earth. If he pins down the mine's location, he's got a long hard ride ahead of him; when he gets to it, he's going to need the right men to do the hard work.'

Liquid splashed as Dark poured another drink. He looked questioningly at King, refilled his glass at the man's nod.

'Let me get this right,' he said carefully. 'You're in a desperate race with the man who stole your property by cheating at cards. You figure if you get to this mine first you can do whatever's necessary to reclaim ownership. My actions facing down those two clowns caught your eye. You figure you stand more chance of success with me alongside you than on your own. For that service my reward is — what?'

'Fifty per cent of the mine's profits.'

'Tempting, but I'd find the story easier to swallow if I was talking to a man in a fancy suit, a gold watch on his vest, drinking champagne out of a crystal glass.'

'I had riches in my grasp, and they were snatched away from me. The gambler who did that, and the man who rides with him, are the hardest men I've ever met — until today. That's where you come in.'

'You might be pinning your faith on a kid who got lucky,' Dark said. 'From what you saw, in here and out there in the street, you know that about me. No more, no less.'

'At my age,' Nathan Kind said, 'judging character becomes a way of life.'

'And you reckon you can reach the mine ahead of this gambler?'

'I know where it is, he's still looking.'

'What if he's beaten you to it? What if he's already there?'

'That could depend,' King said, 'on the company I keep.' He smiled enigmatically. Lifted his glass and held it out over the table. 'I've said enough, you know all there is to know. Are you in, or out?'

Johnny Dark hesitated for but a moment.

'I'm in,' he said, and he lifted his drink to seal the contract in the musical clink of glass.

3

The sun's red disc had slipped behind the purple hills when Johnny Dark said goodnight to Nathan King, left the saloon and crossed the street. The light from hanging lanterns creaking in the night breeze spilled across dust cut by horses' hoofs and pitted with drops of freshly spilled blood.

Dark sprang up onto the far plank walk, turned to his right, walked past the open door of the rooming-house and a further fifty yards to the livery barn. Beyond the barn, a gunsmith's shop was set back from the rest of the buildings. Further up the street, a single oil lamp hung outside the only stone building in town: the Del Rio bank.

Inside the livery barn the runway was dim and cool. Dark's blue roan was in one of the stalls. It heard him, caught his scent and whickered. Dark called softly to it, glanced at the rail where his McLellan saddle gleamed lustrously, then walked through dry rustling straw to the ladder and creaked his way up to the loft. His bedroll and saddle-bags lay against the wall at the street end of the barn. He had ridden into town two days ago. This would be his second night sleeping rough.

Rough?

He smiled into the darkness, stripped his gunbelt from around his waist and hung it on an iron nail hammered into one of the roof joists. Then he dropped to his blankets, carefully rolled and lit a cigarette and stretched out with a grunt of satisfaction.

No, this could not be called rough. Rough was what he'd had for the first ten years of his life in southern Texas, when poverty and grinding hard work had been his legacy after his father had walked away from the family when his son was just two years old. A time best forgotten.

Smooth was a better way of describing the *next* ten years: when his mother died, a sad and lonely woman without a friend in the world, Dark had been forced to leave their home and fend for himself. The qualities that had eased his passage through the wildest regions of the West had been forged by an iron will out of an inner core of steel, honed on insults directed at his dark hair and eyes, at the high cheekbones and hooked nose shaping his lean face.

When muscles hardened and he acquired the stature of a man, long hours of practice had honed his skills with a six-gun. The blurring speed of his slim hands had become legendary, and in confrontations not of his making he had been forced to kill, or die. He faced each fresh challenge with excitement that was like a fever, yet afterwards drew no comfort from his extraordinary prowess. And he had never understood why men would step out into the blazing sun to challenge an unknown kid of slight build as if besting him somehow added to their own reputations.

Until today.

That goddamn air about him, that look in his eyes . . .

Through dedication he had created lightning fast hands that dealt death as swiftly and dispassionately as a riverboat gambler deals cards. That awesome power had become evident in his demeanour. Unconsciously flaunted, it had become an unspoken challenge. Each hothead confronted and brushed aside added to the aura of invincibility that brought a fresh wave of hopefuls willing to risk their lives —

Out in the street, a man coughed.

Set into the wall alongside Dark's blankets there was a wooden double door high above the street. It was bolted shut, but the timber had dried and warped. Dark rolled onto his knees, pressed his face against the door and squinted through a gap between the rough boards.

Moonlight bathed the street in cold light. The gaunt gunslinger was standing at the edge of the shadows on the far plank walk. He was looking across at the livery barn. A cigarette glowed in his cupped left hand. The right arm injured by Dark was in a sling. The light of the moon glinted on the six-gun that was now butt-forward on his right hip to facilitate an awkward, left-handed cross draw.

As Dark watched, the big Mexican stepped out of the shadows behind the gaunt man. He was hatless, unsteady on his feet. Strands of greasy black hair poked from between swathes of white bandages.

A shotgun, cracked at the breech, was folded across his crooked right arm.

The gaunt man's head lifted. Reflected moonlight gave him the milky eyes of a blind man. Those blind eyes appeared to be staring directly at Dark. Then the gunslinger sent his cigarette sparking into the dust. He stepped down into the street. The Mexican snapped the shotgun shut, lifted it to the port arms postion and followed the lean man.

Dark rolled away from the door. He

stood up, unhooked his gunbelt from the nail. Unhurriedly he buckled it around his waist. Then he again peered through the crack.

Both men had almost reached the centre of the street.

Dark was disturbed, but not unduly worried. There were two ways into the loft: through the bolted double doors high above the street — no easy way up, no way in — or by climbing the ladder from the runway. They were making for the runway, and the ladder. If Dark stepped away from the double doors he could melt into the shadows. He could sit tight and listen to the ladder creaking under their weight. When the first man poked his head into the loft he'd be at Dark's mercy, a sitting duck blinking sightlessly at certain death.

All right. If that was what they wanted.

Thinking had taken mere fractions of a second. Again Dark put his eye to the crack in the timber. As he did so, a match flared bright in the shadows on the far sidewalk. Fifty yards down the street, a man had lit a cigarette. Dark frowned, and flicked his gaze back to the two gunslingers. In the centre of the street both men had stopped, alerted by the snap of the match on the man's thumbnail. They swung around. The gaunt man's left hand went to the holster on his right hip.

Both men were both staring at the far sidewalk.

A pinprick of light glowed red as the unseen man drew on his cigarette. There was no movement. From Dark's position he could not be seen. But the two gunslingers were reacting to his presence. The gaunt man's hand lifted clear of his holster. He hooked his thumb into his gunbelt. Shook his head slowly. Alongside him, the Mexican spat into the dust. Then his right hand grasped the shotgun's muzzle and he lifted the double-barrelled weapon and rested it with the trigger guard on his shoulder. Without a word, the two men swung away and walked off down the street.

Nathan King stepped out of the shadows.

His black hat was pulled low. He watched the two men until they cut across to the rooming house. Then he turned, looked up at the double doors where Dark knelt, watching — and he reached up and touched the brim of his hat.

Then he, too, turned and walked away into the night.

★ ★ ★

Over breakfast the next morning — ham and eggs eaten in the smoky atmosphere of the café situated between the rooming house and the livery barn and washed down by several cups of strong black coffee — Johnny Dark had time for some more serious thinking.

Last night, in the time it had taken him to walk from the saloon to the livery barn, he had decided that he didn't believe a word of the older man's story. Nevertheless, although the tale

31

was verging on the preposterous, Dark had nothing better to do and was willing to go along for the ride.

However, the unusual events that had occurred later that same night had provided him with more serious questions, and no answers.

Inside the saloon, Dark had used speed and the unexpected to shock the big Mexican and drop him in the sawdust. The gaunt man had thrown down a challenge; to overcome a dangerous opponent, Dark had been forced to use all his gun fighting skills. Both the Mexican and the gaunt gunslinger had displayed raw, reckless courage. Yet a couple of hours later, Nathan King had forced the two men to put aside their weapons and walk away. He had done nothing more than stand in deep shadows and reveal his face in the flare of a match's flame.

What kind of a man was this? Had the two roughnecks recognized qualities in King that had gone unnoticed by Dark? Or, worse, were they working with King? Had the incidents in the saloon and the street been some kind of a test that had gone horribly wrong for the two men? Was King luring Dark into some deadly game with the promise of riches that existed only in his imagination? But if so, what was that game? And why ensnare Dark, a young man with nothing to offer but deadly proficiency with a six-gun?

Dark was still considering those questions and more over his third cup of coffee when the door clattered open and Nathan King walked in. He tipped his black hat to the café's aproned owner, sniffed deeply of the grease-larded air, and dropped into the seat opposite Dark.

'I detect a whiff of suspicion,' he said. 'You about to walk out on me?'

'And ride away from a fortune?' Dark chuckled. 'Order your breakfast, eat. Then we'll look to mounts, grub, whatever else we need for wherever it is we're going — because, as I recall, that's something you neglected to tell me.'

King shook his head. 'I was in here enjoying an after-breakfast cigarette when you were crawling out of your blankets. I took a list to the general store, supplies are ready on the gallery. There's a pack mule in the livery barn. And if you haven't got the sense to figure out where we're goin', then maybe I picked the wrong man after all.'

'This is Del Rio, Mexico's across the Rio Bravo, and if you really have got yourself a gold mine then it's a toss up between Sierra Madre and the Serranías del Burro.' Dark met the other man's eyes. 'And from what I witnessed last night,' he said, 'I'd say the last thing you need is the assistance of any man, right or wrong.'

King, his grey eyes showing not a flicker of emotion, refused to be drawn.

'You finished?'

'Breakfast — or asking tricky questions?'

34

King scowled and scraped his chair back. 'Come on, let's get out of here, go get that mule.'

Dark followed him out into the street. They stood for a moment in the bright sunlight, adjusting hats, hitching gunbelts, idly watching the increasing bustle of horsemen and creaking wagons pulling clouds of dust, shop-keepers flinging their doors wide for the day's business. Across the street, the Mexican and the tow-headed man with his arm in a sling were deep in conversation with the aproned saloon-ist. He had been wielding a mop and bucket. As he saw Dark and King emerge from the café he nudged the lean man, then picked up the bucket and pitched the filthy water into the street.

The three men were still watching as Dark and King walked the short way up the street to the livery barn.

'I guess they don't scare that easy after all,' Dark said.

This time King limited his response

to a grunt, and pushed on into the livery barn's shadowy runway.

Half an hour later they were outside Del Rio's general store. The mule was loaded with provisions. Dark's blue roan and King's frisky bay mare had their heads up sniffing the warming air. While King finished off inside the store, Dark gave the roan's cinch a final check. He was all done and ready to go when King emerged from the store with several cartons of ammunition and stowed them in the mule's pack.

'And still they watch,' Dark said softly, glancing back up the street. 'Doesn't their interest cause you concern?'

'It might have done if I hadn't got a fast gun on the payroll.'

Dark grinned. 'You never did answer. Which is it, Sierra Madre or the Serranías?'

'They're one and the same,' King said. 'Sierra Madre Oriental stretches all the way from the Stockton Plateau in Texas to Monterrey. But up at that top end, part of the Serranías del Burro, there's the Sierra del Carmen — and that, my boy, is where we're headed.'

'We're heading into the unknown,' Dark said, swinging into the saddle, 'and he's hired a *boy* to do a man's job.'

'You'll handle it,' King said gruffly and, as the older man climbed aboard the bay, Dark was puzzled to observe him turn his head away so that Dark could not see his grey eyes.

Then, without a backward glance at the watching gunslingers, they rode out of Del Rio.

4

They crossed the Rio Bravo before noon, rattled through Ciudad Acuna's somnolent streets of low, white adobe dwellings and pointed their mounts due west. The sun was high and hot, dust already a problem. Both men had bandannas covering the lower half of their faces, hat brims pulled down to protect their eyes as they squinted ahead at a landscape of coarse grass and parched earth stretching ahead to the jagged peaks of the sierras.

With the mule holding them back they had covered no more than fifty miles when the sun sank behind the western mountains. They camped for the night in a grove of trees alongside a stony creek, slept through the hours of darkness and were in the saddle before daybreak to resume the hard push towards the western mountains.

King told Johnny Dark they would reach their destination before nightfall. Those words, spoken almost as a casual aside soon after they broke camp, were all that passed between them until they slowed to a walk just before noon. As they drank warm water from their bottles while sitting loose and easy in the saddle, Dark took a long hard look in a north-easterly direction.

'We're being followed.'

'Wondered when you'd spot them,' King said. 'You notice anything else?'

Dark stowed his water bottle and rode in silence for a while, casting frequent glances over his shoulder. He let his eyes roam far and wide, ignoring the patiently plodding pack mule as he watched the slender plume of dust that drifted lazily in the still air.

'They're holding station,' he said eventually. 'Not getting closer, not falling behind.'

'So what does that tell us?'

'The card sharp who got his thieving hands on a scrap of paper worth a fortune is letting you lead him to the gold.'

King pulled the mare back so he was closer to Dark, and glanced across at his companion.

'That was the easy bit, because we've both been expecting him to appear on the horizon.' He jerked a thumb back over his right shoulder. 'But what about the others?'

The dust cloud that Dark guessed indicated the position of the card sharp who had robbed King was some way to the north-east. But almost directly behind them, a mile or so down their back trail, a second cloud of dust indicated the presence of other riders.

Dark grinned. 'You spotted them, so they're your babies. You tell me.'

'Try this. You made enemies in Del Rio. I think that big Mex and the tow-headed rangy fellow were tipped off by the sharp-eared saloonist. Looks like they're out to settle a score with you, and get rich into the bargain.'

Or maybe not, Dark thought. *Maybe*

they're your compadres, *keeping their distance and a keen eye on the card sharp and his men.*

What he said was, 'If it is those two, and not a bunch of Mexican field hands heading for home, things could get interesting when we reach this mine — if there is a mine.'

'Oh ye of little faith,' King said, shaking his head. 'You're right, though. Those fellows are going to get a big surprise when they find they've got more competition than an old-timer and a kid still wet behind the ears.' He chuckled at that. 'You never can tell, maybe they'll get to fighting so hard amongst themselves they'll forget all about me, and the gold.' Then he shook his head. 'Fat chance of that! Come on, let's you and me kick a little life into the proceedings. If we get where we're going with daylight fading we can really give those greedy *hombres* something to think about.'

He raked the mare with his spurs and flashed Dark a ferocious grin as he set off at a fast canter towards the distant mountains.

★ ★ ★

Dusk was settling over the Mexican landscape like a warm blanket when Dark and King led the laden pack mule into the dry trees and scrub blanketing the northern foothills of the Serranías del Burro and the Sierra del Carmen.

Dark, doing his job, had kept a wary eye on their pursuers. As he had anticipated, the fading light had forced both groups to narrow the gap between them and the men they were following. He had watched this happen with some amusement. Drawing closer to Dark and King had put the two factions on a converging course. Each must now be aware of the other's presence.

Dark put this to his companion.

'So they fight each other, or join forces,' King said, looking back. 'If I know that gambler, he'll promise the earth to the two fellows you bested, then shoot them in the back when he's got his hands on the gold.'

'What they do doesn't change the odds against us,' Dark said. 'We're facing numbers we can't calculate, and we must be getting close to this fabulous mine. What are your plans? Do we stand and fight? You must have had some scheme in mind when you chose to lead your rival all this way.'

Dark, watching King ponder that question, was genuinely intrigued. During most of the ride from Del Rio, King had taken the lead, pushing his bay mare thirty or forty yards ahead of Dark. By doing so, his body had shielded his hands from Dark's view. But Dark had been watching carefully, and several times he had seen the older man looking closely at a folded piece of paper he had taken from his vest pocket.

A man familiar with his destination might still consult a map to ease his mind, to make sure he hadn't strayed from his route, but King, by doing it stealthily, had added to Dark's suspicions. His stories sounded plausible, but they were his stories, issuing from his lips and so far uncorroborated. He had told Dark he had been robbed, cheated out of what was rightfully his — but Dark was well aware that the papers for the mine could belong to the man now trailing them, stolen from him by King, who was being protected by the gunfighters Dark had humbled.

But if the truth lay closer to that version of the story, what did King want from Dark? Why split a fortune into quarters, rather than thirds?

'We lead them a dance,' King said now. 'What else did you expect?'

'Something better. Dancing gets us nowhere if they're still there when the music stops playing.'

King chuckled. 'Be patient. What matters now is keeping ahead.'

With that said, they pushed on.

Gradually the terrain became more rugged. The slopes on their northern flank reared more steeply and climbed to ever higher crags. Coarse grass was sparse on the rocky trail, now made treacherous by the twisted roots of parched trees searching for water, by deep gullies gouged out of the earth when winter rains tumbled down the mountainside.

As he sat back in the saddle and let the roan pick its surefooted way along the rocky trail, Dark listened grimly as the iron of their horses' shoes rang out in the darkness. He knew those musical signals that drew bright sparks from the stone would send a clear message to the men riding hotly in pursuit.

Those followers would be getting anxious. The light had almost gone. If they were not to lose their quarry, the two groups who had spent a long day hanging back would now need to ride to within earshot. They would hear the ring of horseshoes, but that they were able to do so carried its own risks: sound carried in all directions. So they were forced to ride close, yet while doing so they must strive to say undetected.

'If they tie sacking over their horses' hoofs, we won't hear them until they're on us,' Dark said.

'Forget it.' King was riding a few yards in front of him, the bay picking its way up a steep, winding slope. 'Their minds are filled with greed, not ideas of stealth. We're that close to the mine they've got nothing to lose.'

'They don't know that.'

'I wouldn't bank on it. They know there's easier ways of getting places. Only one reason I'd take this godforsaken trail. That's because somewhere close there's a hole in the hillside and it's full of precious metal.'

'Where?'

King chuckled. 'We've already left it behind us.'

Dark grunted in surprise.

They rode on without speaking for another half-hour, both men clinging to their saddle horns as the horses swayed and stumbled, Dark hanging on to the lead-rope as the tired pack mule began to lag. Several times King turned to grin at Dark as a horse whickered faintly somewhere behind them, or they heard the distant rattle of a dislodged stone bounding down a wooded slope.

King's admission that they had passed the mine told Dark that the older man had indeed been looking at his crumpled piece of paper merely for confirmation: even in the dark he knew exactly where he was. But was that because the mine truly had been stolen from him? Or was it because he was at home in this part of Mexico, had long known of the mine, and deliberately set out to steal it?

Those questions were still occupying Dark's thoughts when he realized with a jolt that the land had flattened somewhat and King was pulling off the trail. A crescent moon had floated into cloudless skies, throwing the high crags into relief. By its wan light Dark saw his companion push the bay up a steep bank, take it on and over and through the trees, then draw to a halt.

'I'll tie the animals, you get a fire

going,' King said, as Dark joined him. 'Do it fast. Before long they'll realize we've stopped. I want them to see that fire blazing, figure we've made camp for the night.'

'Have we?'

'Not yet,' King said. 'And not here.'

The timber all about them was dry. Dark found kindling, branches, piled the lot into a crude circle of stones and within minutes flames were banishing the shadows and flickering on the encircling trees.

The animals secured, King joined him, and quickly got coffee brewing in a blackened pot suspended over the flames. The aroma of hot java soon had Dark's mouth watering, but over the bubbling of the coffee and the crackle of the flames he was struggling to listen for the sound of movement in the surrounding woods.

'Rest easy,' King said, watching him. 'The idea is we put them at their ease thinking we're here for the night. Unroll some blankets. Douse the fire so there's not much light. And then after a while has passed, we walk away.'

'Walk?' Dark set two mugs upright close to the blaze, wrapped his bandanna around his hand and poured coffee from the hot pot. 'We rode for a half-hour *after* you said we'd passed the mine. If that's where we're going, it'll take half the night.'

'We rode for thirty minutes in a half circle. Now we're going to walk for ten minutes in that direction.' King jerked a thumb over his shoulder.

Dark carefully sipped the scalding hot coffee, then shook his head.

'I don't get it. Why? What are we doing? We leave horses and equipment here and walk away — where's the sense in that?'

'Nothing we've done so far,' King said, 'will have made much sense to you. On the surface it looks like we've been leading a bunch of greedy gamblers and gunslingers in a wild race across the desert looking for a gold mine that might exist only in my imagination. But things are rarely as they seem, and up to now you've gone along with everything I've done. You've done that because I promised you a share in those riches. Well, I can tell you — I have told you — we're getting very close. What are you going to do now, throw your share away because the step I'm proposing — which could be the final step — makes no damn sense?'

Dark smiled. 'That's a long speech,' he said, 'when all I said was I don't get it.'

'Long speeches are what I do, when I'm in the mood,' King said, 'and there's nothing quite like cash money for putting me there.'

They spent the next couple of hours sitting by the fire listening to the logs settling, the coffee pot singing, the soft sighing of the warm night wind across the tops of the tall trees, the occasional crack of a twig out in the woods caused by a movement too clumsy for any animal.

Between cups of coffee, King told

50

Dark that before too long the men watching them would reach the desired conclusion and slip away through the woods to make their own camp.

Dark held no opinion on the matter. The remark that had brought a long verbal reaction from King had been said to keep the conversation alive, to pass the time. Nevertheless, King's reply had been interesting. It suggested that even to the older man the story he had told Dark seemed preposterous.

So Dark sat, and waited.

Finally, with the hour approaching ten, King grunted, planted his empty cup in the grey ash at the edge of the fire, and climbed to his feet.

'Time,' he said quietly. 'Let's go to bed.'

He winked at Dark, used his boot to scrape dirt over the fire until it was almost smothered. The moon had drifted across the sky to be hidden by the trees. With the flames gone the small clearing was in darkness.

Moving swiftly, Dark slipped silently

to where the animals were tethered. He slid his Winchester from its boot, patted his thigh to check that his six-gun was settled in its holster.

Then King was with him. He handed over a gunny sack that Dark sensed contained water bottles, jerky, shells for rifle and pistol. Then he touched Dark's shoulder, and walked away into the woods.

King had said ten minutes at most. They struggled uphill for fifty yards, then cut across the rounded flank of the hill. The woods were thick, but the walking was easy. Dead leaves underfoot were a soft carpet, muffling sound. Dark kept King in sight, but not too close. Something told him the time had come. Whatever was going to happen would happen very soon. If it involved this man, then Dark wanted space between them.

Like King, he had heard no sounds for some time. But something else King had said was that things are rarely as they seem. So Dark continued to listen

— and heard nothing. It was as if they were alone in the woods. Two men in search of a gold mine.

Or maybe not.

As Dark smiled at his own doubts, he saw King suddenly turn into the hillside — and disappear. Dark stopped. He waited for several heartbeats. His breathing was shallow. Every sense was tuned to what lay around him, or ahead.

Then King reappeared. He looked towards Dark, and waved him on.

When Dark walked the twenty yards or so that separated them, King's disappearance was explained. Their walk had brought them to a man-made clearing bathed in light from the crescent moon. Dark saw a rough rectangular opening in sheer cliffs. It was braced by rotting timber props. Soil that had been dug from the bowels of the earth lay everywhere in mounds. More ancient props braced the crumbling roof of the tunnel that seemed to burrow deep into the hillside.

Dark looked at King, and nodded.

'OK. So far so good.'

King grinned. 'And now your work begins.'

'Doing what?'

'Nothing at all.'

Dark sighed. 'Always the joker. Always one jump ahead, keeping me guessing. All right, if I do nothing — what about you?'

'The nearest town is Pueblo Pequeño. Twenty miles away. I can be there tonight, hire workers in the early morning, be back here by noon tomorrow.'

'You'd put your trust in Mexicans?'

'I'd put my trust in almost anyone, except Indians. Indians are bloodthirsty savages. Mexicans work hard — '

'So why don't we both ride to this village?'

'With two factions on our tail? If they join forces when they came together, they can just as easily split. One group following us, one searching for the mine. And if that second group gets lucky . . . '

54

'They can still split. And the ones who remain behind *might* get lucky.'

'But they won't know I have gone. And if they find out, and the second group does succeed in finding this mine — *then* your work begins.'

'This is what you hired me for? I hold off an army while you sit in the sun drinking mescal?'

'I'll be doing that, sure, at a table in the town's *cuadrado*, the square; and as I drink my drink and puff on a fat cigar, the villagers, the *aldeanos*, will be lining up for work. *That* will be an army. Good enough to make the rabble out there turn tail and run.'

It was a statement that was unexpected; Dark was impressed. Not with the truth, but with the lies. Nathan King didn't know when to stop. He told a good story, then ruined it by exaggeration. But what the *hell* was he up to?

'It still sounds good,' Dark said. He tossed the sack of supplies into the mouth of the mine, and nodded at

King. 'Ride into town, hire your workers. One way or another, you'll see me tomorrow.'

'You mean dead or alive?' King grinned. 'I didn't hire you to get killed.'

He stepped forward, arms flung wide. For a brief moment he embraced Dark, enfolding him in a mighty bear hug. Then he turned and walked away into the woods.

5

Some way to the north-east the four trail-weary riders following Nathan King and Johnny Dark were coming in cagily from the barren slopes of the plains, walking their horses with care into the first of the trees blanketing the foothills.

As Dark had predicted, they had closed the gap between pursued and pursuers when the light began to fail. But these were men experienced in hunting down fugitives from the law. The long chase would inevitably end in violent confrontation, but that confrontation would be on their terms, and at a time of their choosing.

The man leading the single file of riders was spare and dark-featured. He was astride a small, wiry dun mare. A plug of tobacco bulged in his unshaven cheek. His dark eyes were restless, and his sharp ears were listening constantly to the faint sounds drifting back to him from the fugitives: the crack of a branch, the rattle of a stone; the faint yet unmistakable snort of a horse.

On this man's vest, a badge glittered.

'Pueblo Pequeño,' he said. 'The Mex town's where he's headed, that's where we'll take him.'

The burly man riding behind him on the tough little paint stifled a cough with his hand.

'King, on his own, we can handle,' he said. 'But what about this other fellow riding with him? The kid who rode into Del Rio, bested a Mexican and a fast Texas gunny, then spent a half hour talking to King in the saloon.'

'Is that what happened?'

'According to the town marshal, Clarence Fogg, that's *exactly* what happened. Today, King and that kid rode out together, they're up ahead of us, and so I'd very much like to know more about this kid who's a mite too fast and accurate with his six-gun.'

58

'I can't help you because I *don't* know him, don't know anything about him.'

'That's what I'm getting at, Marshal. This unknown kid presents a risk that wasn't there before King rode out of Del Rio. What if this brash kid's dictating tactics? What if he's smart enough to turn a simple bank robber into a soldier capable of winning battles?'

'We're four against two.' Leather creaked as the lawman turned in the saddle, looked back down the short line of riders threading its way through the trees. 'I'd put my trust in every one of you — and the only soldier likely to affect the outcome of this little fracas is me. I did my four years in butternut. If the damn Yankees couldn't put out my light, that cheap thief King stands no chance at all — with or without the help of that young upstart.'

6

It took Dark but a few minutes to prepare himself for what was to come. He began by leaning his Winchester against a tree and tossing the gunny sack into the mine entrance. Then he looked around for stout logs, and rocks that had fallen from the over-hanging cliffs. Using these he built a rampart, a low but solid barrier behind which he could take cover. Then he took a last look around, picked up his rifle and stepped inside his fortress.

The thin crescent moon lit up the area from which the trees had been cleared. If men launched an attack, from any direction, they would be seen. But the open area was no more than thirty yards deep from trees to mine. A quick sprint would carry men across it in under five seconds. They would be in the open, and Dark's field of fire was almost 180 degrees — but achieving the limits of that arc would leave him, too, dangerously exposed.

He was checking the loads of both rifle and six-gun when he heard the sound of hoofbeats, fast receding. He smiled grimly. A man playing a stealthy game against dangerous opponents would have led his horse away at a walk until out of earshot. King, it seemed, had mounted up and ridden off at a gallop — and to hell with the consequences.

But what were the consequences?

That, Dark knew, depended on the nature of the game being played by Nathan King. If the man was genuine, then by riding off in haste he had slipped up badly and it could cost him dear. On the other hand, if every word he had spoken was a lie, the consequences would be the achievement of his goal — whatever that might be.

For Dark, whether by accident or design, those consequences were likely to be disastrous. And he was still mentally berating himself for his own stupidity when the first shot rang out and a slug ricocheted with a vicious whine from the roof of the mine.

★ ★ ★

The muzzle flash had come from the woods to Dark's left. He grabbed his rifle and snapped a hasty shot in that direction. At once a volley of shots poured at him from both flanks. Dark dropped flat behind his solid rampart. Bullets whanged off stone walls and roof. Splinters of rock hissed. A needle-sharp fragment hit his cheek and he felt the hot trickle of blood.

The firing stopped. Silence fell. Dark's ears rang. His pulse was hammering. Cautiously he came up on his knees. He tossed his hat away and sneaked a look over the top of the low wall. Gunsmoke was still drifting like mist on the fringes of the woods.

Coolly, methodically, using the rifle, Dark stitched a line of bullets along the length of the trees. He did it fast, placing the shots ten yards apart. Then he ducked back down.

Seconds dragged by. He thought he heard voices. Guessed that the attackers were discussing what to do next. If they were here at King's bidding, he had left them unprepared. They had expected to encounter a skilful gunman, but Dark's position was causing them problems.

Dark couldn't see why. Military men would lay down a blanket of fire and send an assault force in under its cover. He would be forced to keep his head down. In the five seconds it took attackers to cross that open ground, it would be all over.

The silence crawled on. Dark felt a cold worm of perspiration wriggle down his back. He closed his eyes. His hands were sweaty, slippery on the rifle's stock, on its barrel. He wiped each palm on his pants in turn. Again checked his pistol.

Then the barrage began. But now

there was a surprise for Dark. Just one rifleman was firing, and he was on the right flank. One rifleman — but a rifleman firing with deadly accuracy. Bullets thudded into the ramparts. Others clipped splinters from the logs. One kicked a shower of dirt into Dark's face. He twisted away, scrubbing at his burning eyes.

Suddenly the rifleman shifted his aim. Now his shots were all aimed high. They were hammering into the cliff face, howling off the mine's roof, ricocheting down the tunnel with rapidly fading whines. With dismay, Dark realized what that meant. His eyes watering, he lifted his head and risked a look.

And got another surprise.

From the centre of the trees, a man was charging across the open ground. He ran half crouched, keeping beneath the covering fire. And again it was just that — one man, when Dark had been expecting several. Where the hell where the others? What were they doing? Dark stood up, stepped back into the shadows. The incoming fire was high, he thought he was safe — but he had nowhere to go.

Suddenly there was a terrible, tearing pain in his left hand. He lifted it, stared in shock. The hand was in spasm, trembling uncontrollably. A stray bullet had ripped off three of his fingers. Blood was dripping onto his leg. He cursed softly through gritted teeth. The wound was agony. Pain was like a hot iron piercing his arm from hand to shoulder. His head swam. He staggered backwards, tossed the rifle aside, wrapped the fingers of his right hand round his wrist and tightened his grip.

Mere seconds had passed. The rifleman on the right flank continued to pour bullets into the mine. The advancing gunslinger had almost made it across the open ground. From the corner of his eye Dark could see the man's pistol, held high, glittering in the moonlight.

Now he was just ten feet away. Uncertain, wary, he had slowed, stopped.

Dark took a deep, shuddering breath. Again he lifted his bloody left hand. Gingerly he eased it inside his shirt, used the buttoned shirt as a sling. Then he drew his pistol. Cocked it. Placed his back flat against the cold stone wall.

Heart thundering, teeth bared in pain, Johnny Dark prepared to die fighting.

PART TWO

7

1895

It was late afternoon when the man rode up to the small tin-roofed cabin on the western outskirts of Laredo. He had a six-gun at his hip, a Winchester in the saddle boot under his right thigh. In the fading sunlight the badge on his vest glinted like gold.

He was a tall man riding a magnificent white horse. His hair was worn quite long, as black as an Indian's. His cheekbones were high, his skin tanned. But his eyes were as blue as the summer skies reflected in the waters of the Rio Grande, and when he drew rein and swung from the saddle those eyes were dancing with barely suppressed excitement.

The appetizing aroma of hot dinner was in his nostrils as he pushed through the front door into the cabin's single living room. Mouth already watering he paused there, cast those blue eyes across the neat timber furniture, the table with its red-and-white checked cloth and dishes neatly laid for two.

The young woman was watching him from the stove. Her dark eyes were dancing. But her obvious delight at seeing him was tempered by uncertainty and a burning curiosity.

'You're home early today.'

'What I have to tell you couldn't wait.'

'So . . . '

He grinned at his wife, a flash of white teeth.

'Well, perhaps it can wait a little longer. Until I've washed and eaten.'

'I'll put the dinner out.'

He touched her gently in passing, took hold of her shoulders and kissed the nape of her neck. He felt her lean into him for a moment, a warm, slim young woman in fitted denim trousers and work shirt, her long hair tied back, her skin fresh, a young woman strong in both body and mind; his rock, the woman who sustained him. Then he went on through and out the back door. There was a tin wash bowl there, and an iron water pump. He swilled his face and hands in ice-cold water, then took his time drying himself on the towel hanging on a nail hammered into the back wall. All the while, his thoughts were churning.

When he returned to the living-room his dinner was out, the heaped plates on the table: meat and root vegetables, a rich dark gravy; next to the plate thick slices of rye bread in a basket.

'So,' the woman said some long, quiet minutes later, 'has this news now waited long enough?'

'More than enough. *I*'ve waited long enough. No — I've waited much *too* long. And so . . . '

He pushed his empty plate away and sat back. He was conscious of her watching him intently. Without ceremony he reached up to the gleaming badge, unpinned it, and placed it on the table in front of him.

'I resigned today. Left my job.'

The woman sighed. Closed her eyes. When she opened them again there was reproof in them, and a glimmer of anger.

'Are we back to that again?'

'Yes. That again. For, what, the hundredth time? The thousandth? Surely more times than I can count, but this time, Cath, I cannot make it go away.'

'Why not? You're twenty-six years old, a deputy town marshal — '

'I was — '

' — and everyone is saying that when Will retires the top job will be yours. He's old now — and soon you'll be town marshal. Why walk away?'

'Because I need to know,' he said simply.

'No, that's just it, after all this time, after five long *years* you *don't* need to know.'

'All right, then for my peace of mind I *want* to know. If my mind is at rest then we'll both be settled, we can start raising a family — '

'You don't mean that.'

He smiled. 'Yes. I do. Of course I mean it, and you know we'll be wonderful parents. I want that completeness as much as you do — but it has to be *afterwards*.'

She uttered a soft murmur of frustration, pushed away from the table and poured two cups of coffee. When she sat down with them her cheeks were pink. Again he was aware of her watching him, this time from under lowered lashes, obviously holding her temper in check. Watching, and waiting.

But for what, he wondered? Did she expect him to change his mind? He knew he couldn't do that, not after today. Not after facing Will, after telling the old lawman what he intended to do. After receiving the old man's approval, his good wishes, the offer of help which he had turned down. Well, tried to turn down, he thought, smiling inwardly.

Oh, he could see the apprehension

and anger in his wife's dark eyes. Natural apprehension, justifiable anger. Which he understood. But there was no need for it. Because . . .

'Cath,' he said, reaching across the table to touch her hand. 'Cath, I want you to go with me.'

She looked up quickly, her gaze startled.

'Go with you? But . . . I'm a woman.' Realizing what she had said, knowing that with her obvious strengths the remark had been ridiculous, she shook her head in exasperation. 'Wouldn't I be in the way; in your way?'

Now he shook his head. 'Your pa taught you to shoot. You have your own pistol. You can ride as well as any man. And I'm going to need someone with me, someone I can trust.'

'You would worry too much. In a tight situation your thoughts would be with me, your *concern* would be for me — and that could be fatal, for you, for me . . . '

'Cath,' he said softly, 'I *need* you. You

are part of me, without you — '

He broke off as she left the table and whirled to stand with her back to him, her arms folded. He rose, too, and went to her. He took her in his arms and let her turn within his embrace so that she was facing him, her eyes on his, her breath warm on his face.

'I'd like that,' she said, her eyes challenging. 'Oh, I really would like that, riding with you, *helping* you. But I want you to promise me' — she reached for his hand, took hold of it firmly, touched with tenderness the knuckles from which the three fingers had been so cruelly severed — 'I want you to promise me that if things look like going wrong again, if there comes a point when it's obvious that finding out is not worth the price you must pay — then this time you will walk away. We will walk away. Walk away — and come home to raise that family.'

'That's an easy one,' Johnny Dark said, 'because it's what I always promised myself I would do.'

'So . . . if that's it all settled, when do we ride?'

'Tomorrow.'

'My word,' Cath Dark said, eyes wide. 'After the hundredth or thousandth time of thinking about it and getting nowhere, suddenly he's impulsive.'

'More like reckless,' Dark said. 'I've been putting it off for five years. Now I've made the decision, I'm scared to death it's the wrong one and I'll live to regret it.'

That was what he told his wife. What he was thinking — sombrely, and with deep misgivings he was striving to overcome — was that the decision he was beginning to regret could just as easily leave him dead.

8

On the banks of the Rio Grande a mile south of Del Rio the hot wind was blowing hard from the east, rustling through the brittle leaves of the cotton-woods, causing the loose slat on the side of the rundown cabin to slap monotonously.

Two horses dozed in the small corral behind the cabin. Their saddles hung over the corral's top rail. In front of the cabin a single horse was tied to the hitch rail. It was saddled. Its flanks were quivering. Traces of white lather showed on its neck, and beneath the faded saddle blanket.

Nathan King, thin and pale, was standing on the gallery gazing out at the dust blowing along the river. A big Mexican with the scar slicing through the stubble on his jaw was sitting on the dry grass with his fat back against one of the trees, his sombrero tilted over his eyes. A tall blond man with a crooked right arm was walking towards the gallery. His eyes were narrowed against the midday sun as he looked towards King.

He got as far as the steps, sat down heavily, wiped the sweat from his brow.

'Did that wire tell you anything worth knowing?'

'Plenty,' King said, glancing down at him. 'That's a good friend I've got in Laredo. Knows a lot. He reckons a deputy by the name of Dark has given up his job so's he can head north. Seems he's ... er ... looking for a man.'

'How does that affect us?'

'Us?' King laughed shortly. 'Hell, I used you two once before, and look where it got me.'

'No, you look at what it got me,' the blond said, and he lifted his crooked right arm.

'Don't blame me for that,' King said. 'You were supposed to leave Dark

78

alone. I wanted him out there' — he nodded across the river — 'but the minute the kid steps inside the saloon Pascal goes up close behind him and gets his damn fool head cracked open, then you call him out into the street and make a fool of yourself.'

'Tombs just asked you how the news you got affects us,' the Mexican drawled, not shifting the big hat. 'So what are you saying now? Because of what happened five years ago, you can do without our help?'

'What happened five years ago was you let me down here, in Del Rio — then like a fool I trusted you to finish a job out there at Pueblo Pequeño, and you let Dark slip through your fingers.'

The blond man called Tombs kicked angrily at a step.

'It got too quiet after the shooting. We waited until first light. When we looked inside that mine there was blood, a lot of blood — but no sign of Dark.'

'There was no other way out. You

should have gone in there after him.'

Pascal's voice was cold. 'It would take more than a desire to please you,' he said, 'to get me one inch inside that godforsaken hole.'

King snorted in disgust. 'You spend too much time over there listening to Antonio's superstitious friends.' He looked across at the Mexican. 'How is he, anyway? How is Antonio these days?'

'Unchanged,' Pascal said, flipping back the sombrero. He grinned, his black eyes mocking. 'He is the same handsome man, no paler, no thinner . . .'

'Yeah,' King said bitterly, 'but then he hasn't wasted the last five years.' He glared at Pascal. 'But that's not what I meant. I need to know if he's ready.'

'Sure,' Pascal said, 'Antonio is *always* ready.'

'Which brings us right back to where we were,' Tombs cut in. 'We can make up for everything, today, tomorrow, make up for all that time you lost — all we need is the word from you.'

'You'll get the word when Dark rides into town,' King said. 'I'll talk to him. Tell him something that'll shock the hell out of him — and then we'll move, *then* we'll do it.'

'And when it's over, when the job is done, you are convinced Dark will follow,' Pascal said, 'because of this shock you deliver?'

'He'd follow anyway,' King said with absolute conviction. 'But what I tell him when we talk will have him trotting after me like a day-old calf after its ma.'

He stood straight, stretched, yawned.

'There's another thing my friend in Laredo told me,' he said. 'When John Dark rides north, his wife is riding with him. The damn fool kid's playing right into my hands.'

9

They rode away from their Laredo home when the sun was still a thin strip of gold across the eastern horizon, the mist hanging flat over the Rio Grande, their horses' breath pluming white in the chill air.

Travelling light with provisions and the shells for their weapons carried in saddle-bags, they were comforted by the knowledge that the journey north to Del Rio would take them no more than a day and a half. Dark was impatient. The sooner there, the sooner it would be finished — one way or another.

Their pace was brisk without being hurried, and they chose to ride with the big, smooth river that was the border between Texas and Mexico always in sight. During the morning they rode through Colombia and Hidalgo without pause. The long hot afternoon passed without a break. As evening fell, tired and coated with trail dust, they splashed through a ford in the river so that they could spend the night in the Mexican town of Guerrero.

Over supper in a surprisingly hospitable *cantina*, Dark was questioned by Cath about the events of five years ago, but could add little to what she already knew. The disused mine where he had lost his fingers was located in the foothills of the Sierra del Carmen. The small Mexican town nearest to the mine was Pueblo Pequeño. Dark had no idea what had happened to Nathan King when he walked away from the mine, and the identity of the men who had followed them all the way from Texas remained a mystery.

'If King returned to the mine that night,' Cath said, as they walked through the moonlight to their camp in a stand of willows on the banks of the river, 'your disappearance would have been another mystery. He must have seen the shells. There were clear signs of a fierce gunfight. And behind your makeshift barricade there were pools of spilled blood.'

'You're right. If he wanted me dead, the blood was a good sign, but where was the body?'

'If he wanted you dead,' Cath said, 'why go to the bother of taking you in his employ and riding with you all the way to a disused Mexican mine?'

'Why concoct that outrageous story of a mine won and lost on the turn of a card?'

'Why walk away, leaving you at the mine for others to kill?'

'And why, anyway, would he want me dead?' Dark said. 'I saw him for the first time in my life when I walked into that saloon in Del Rio.'

'Many questions to be asked, Deputy,' Cath said, sliding into her blankets.

Dark was sitting cross-legged by his saddle, smoking a last cigarette. For a while he sat listening to the nearby flow of the river, the familiar sounds of the night. Then he drew a deep breath.

'I haven't been absolutely honest,' he said softly into the darkness.

'Not telling me everything you know, or everything you have planned, is not necessarily dishonest. Some things are best kept quiet until the time is right.'

Dark smiled. 'This is about the job. You reminded me by calling me Deputy. I did try to give it up, but Will forced me to keep the badge. For two reasons. The job is there for me, if we ever make it back to Laredo. And having the badge with me provides the back-up for a letter in Will's handwriting that asks the marshal of Del Rio to assist me in any way he can.'

'Oh, my,' Cath said, yawning, 'what wicked lies you do tell, Johnny Dark.'

And as he was dropping off to sleep, Dark was unable to dispel from his thoughts the other secret that he had kept for five years, and the realization that now, at last, he would learn if the promise that secret held was worth the long wait, or as worthless as fool's gold.

The next morning they rode along the Mexican bank of the Rio Grande as far as Piedras Negras. There they crossed the river to Eagle Pass, and pushed on to Quemado. When the sun was directly overhead they drew rein in the shade of cottonwoods, knelt by the river to wash the dust from their faces, then ate a meal of jerky washed down with warm water from their canteens.

By mid-afternoon they were clattering through Jiménez.

They rode into Del Rio, bone-weary, when the sun was dipping behind the peaks of the Sierra Madre. As they had agreed during the final stages of the long ride, Cath went to sign them into the rooming-house close to the livery barn. Dark rode those extra few yards down the street and hitched his white horse in front of the jail.

★ ★ ★

'The Comeback Kid, the fast gun I didn't want in my town.' The marshal of Del Rio was nodding slowly as he looked at Dark. 'Five years is a long time, but I pride myself on never forgetting a face.' He tilted his head, his grey eyes studying Dark critically, but with approval. 'You've changed some.'

'Older?'

'Wiser,' the marshal said. 'I figured you'd go all the way bad, or mend your ways.'

He was a skinny string-bean of a man, face long and mournful, sharp eyes buried in deep, lined hollows. He was sitting behind his desk; he hadn't moved since Dark pushed open the door and walked into the office. A stained Stetson was pushed back on his head exposing thinning grey hair.

On the desk a small, triangular block of wood was burned with the name Clarence Fogg. The keen eyes — noting the direction of Dark's gaze — were amused.

'Don't let that fool you,' he said. 'I

built up a considerable reputation despite bearing names fit for a buffoon. So use your acquired wisdom, get to the point. Tell my why you've disregarded my advice and come back to Del Rio.'

'Your memory's impressive,' Dark said.

'Deductive powers ain't too bad either. You're looking for Nathan King.'

'So . . . is he still here?'

'Oh, he's around.'

'And the two men a twenty-year old kid with fast hands made to look like greenhorns?'

'Them too.'

'Live in town?'

Fogg grinned. 'That'd be too easy.'

'So where?'

The marshal shrugged. 'King's got a shack down-river. The Mex and the gunslinger reside over the border in Ciudad Acuna, cross the river from time to time. Names are Pablo Pascal and Rick Tombs. I'll leave you to fit names to faces.'

'They cross the river to see King?'

'They do now.'

There was something in the marshal's tone that was inviting a question. Dark considered the man's words.

' 'Now' makes it sound like Pascal and Tombs seeing King is something new. Maybe because before now it wasn't possible.' There was no reaction from Fogg, so Dark went on, 'All right, so tell me what King been doing for the past five years.'

'Paying for his sins.'

Dark frowned. 'He's been in jail?'

'Nathan King's spent the past five years in the Texas State Penitentiary. Robbed a bank over in Waco. The posse he thought he could outrun trailed him all the way into Mexico. Unofficially.' Fogg raised an eyebrow. 'But you'd know all about that, you being there at the time.'

'Christ!' Dark shook his head in disbelief. 'Are you saying when I rode off with King we were followed by a posse from Waco?'

'Yep — and that's about all I can say. They caught up with King in Pueblo Pequeño. I never saw hide nor hair of him until recently, never saw you again until today. So maybe you can fill in the gaps. What about you? What have *you* been doing while he's been staring at four walls?'

Dark reached into his vest pocket, took out his gleaming badge and placed it on the desk before Clarence Fogg.

'For the past *four* years I've been deputy marshal in Laredo. But I never could rid my mind of what went on here, the story I was told by Nathan King. I'm not saying I was taken in, but I was young, and I was foolish enough to go along for the ride. It cost me three fingers.' Dark held up his left hand.

'A gunfight? You and King up against the Waco posse?'

Dark shook his head. 'King rode off into the night. I was on my own.'

'Where?'

'A disused gold mine. About twenty miles this side of Pueblo Pequeño.'

'So not the posse, because they would have been chasing King?'

Dark thought for a moment, then nodded.

'Yes. I've got my own ideas about who tried to kill me. But before anything can be confirmed I need to talk to King.'

'A man makes a habit of lying, it's a tough one to break. You expecting to hear the truth?'

'Like you said, I'm older and wiser. The story he told me then has been disproved. He's going to tell the truth, or dream up another story. It should be interesting.'

'No time like the present. Take a walk up the street, you'll find Nathan King in the saloon.'

Fogg climbed to his feet, stretched and yawned. Dark guessed that, for the time being, they'd run out of talk. As he made for the door, the marshal delivered his parting shot, and Dark paused.

'This job gets a mite boring, and a

91

good story always makes my day,' Fogg said. 'I've enjoyed our talk, so be sure to call in again. Before you do, use some of the underhand tricks you must have practised being a lawman down in Laredo. Question King about why he wanted you dead, then come up on his blind side and ask him which bank he plans to rob next.'

* * *

The man with the flat-crowned black hat with a plaited rawhide band, tipped forward, hiding his eyes, was sitting at the same table he had occupied when Dark first saw him five years ago. Dark trod the same path to the bar; ordered the same drink; spun a coin of the same value on the bar's warped boards and turned, as he had done five years ago, to survey the room.

This time, King was looking up. The eyes that would always be as grey as winter were fixed on Dark. Without calling out, he stretched a leg beneath the table and pushed out the opposite chair. A clear invitation.

Up closer, as he placed his drink on the table, Dark could see that the man had aged. Something — shock at the sight of Dark, or the long years in prison — had bleached the colour from his face. The straggly hair poking out from beneath the hat was white.

'You look as if you've seen a ghost.'

'I'm looking at the man I said a prayer for when I was caught cold by a posse. And, yes, you're right — I thought you were dead, son.'

'If you thought that, then you rode away from me knowing what was about to happen — '

'No.'

' — so tell me, who was supposed to fill me full of holes in that mine? The phantom gambler chasing you for a motherlode that doesn't exist? Or Pascal and Tombs?'

'Pascal and Tombs never rode into Mexico. The riders directly behind you and me were a bunch of Mex peasants heading for home.'

'Five years ago that was my suggestion about the other group,' Dark said. 'You're losing your touch, feeding my words back to me.'

'I can't change what happened.'

'No,' Dark said, 'you can't.' He hesitated. 'You've been inside for five years, I've been wearing a deputy's badge in Laredo. I guess that puts us on opposite sides.'

King looked amused. 'I've paid my dues. Besides, there's one damn good reason why you'd never arrest me.'

Dark's smile was cold. 'Don't bank on it.'

'Ain't you going to ask me what that reason is?'

'What I want to know,' Dark said, 'is if the man who stole your mine was in the second bunch of riders we saw to the north east, where was the posse?'

'That second bunch was the posse.'

'So, no gambler, no card sharp.'

'All lies. I admit it now. Damn near everything I told you was untrue.'

Dark nodded, his lips tight with anger. 'Which brings me to the big question. If Pascal and Tombs were back in Del Rio, the gambler doesn't exist and the posse was hot on your heels — why did you pray for me?'

'All right, yes, it was Pascal, it was Tombs. But I prayed for you because I hired you, took you into Mexico, then walked out on you. And right then I *was* telling you the truth. I intended to hire men, return with them to the mine the next day. Through no fault of mine, that didn't work out.'

Dark shook his head in disbelief.

'You mean robbing the bank in Waco had nothing to do with you?'

'Sure, the guilt was all mine, but the timing of my arrest was all wrong.' King shrugged. 'Saying a prayer was the natural thing to do — even if only as a selfish act to ease my conscience.'

'I don't believe that,' Dark said. 'A prayer can ask for many things, and telling me you said one is probably the first time you've told me the truth. But

I think the prayer was against me, not for me. You left me there to die. The posse prevented you getting back to the mine. You were praying your hired killers had finished the job you began in this saloon.'

He drained his glass, watching Nathan King, trying to read the man's eyes. The bank robber had settled back in his chair. He was nodding slowly, lips pursed, the grey eyes distant. Then they focused, and in them Dark saw a decision.

King said, 'Something else discussed that first time here was names. I asked you if a child is somehow bestowed with a name that fits, or grows into it. You said that either way it hadn't worked for me.'

'After what happened,' Dark said, 'the only name that would suit you is Judas.'

King smiled. 'King doesn't, and never will,' he said, 'because that's a name I took for myself when I walked away from my home and my family some twenty-four years ago.'

Dark went cold. It was a confession from a virtual stranger and therefore unimportant — yet even as the words hung in the air Dark's mind was doing the calculations and recoiling from the implications. He felt the icy sweat on his brow, saw Nathan King watching him; swallowed hard, tried to look away . . .

King leaned forward, placed his hands flat on the table, stared directly into Dark's eyes.

'I told you there was a damn good reason why you'd never arrest me, and that reason is because we're kin. *Close* kin. My real name is Thomas Dark. The reason I've called you son so often is because that's what you are. I'm your father, John boy. So now you've got some questions to ask yourself, some deciding to do. Did a father arrange the killing of his own son — or did I take you with me into Mexico because the best part of that story I told you was the honest to goodness truth?'

10

'Why should we believe anything that man tells you?' Cath said softly.

They were eating a hot meal in the diner where, five years ago, Dark had sat talking to the man who called himself Nathan King. Weary from the long ride, hungry for something that had not been coated in dust then cooked and blackened over a smoky desert camp-fire, they were relishing the food that had been placed before them by the perspiring owner.

'We can disregard almost everything,' Dark said, 'but why would he lie about being my father?'

'Liars always have their reasons. You say he sat back, did some thinking. What better way to convince you he hadn't tried to get you killed than by concocting a close relationship?'

'Why bother at all?'

'Because he still needs you, and listening to you he knows he's lost your trust. By making you his son, he hopes to regain it.'

Dark pushed his plate away.

'*Making* me? So you do think he's lying?'

'I don't know.'

'And why would he need me?'

Cath was frowning, her lips pursed. 'He's just got out of jail. Then you ride into town. Suddenly he's where he was five years ago. He implied that the best part of the tale he told you was true. So what if there really is gold in that mine at Pueblo Pequeño?'

Memory flared like an ember fanned by the wind, and Dark quickly looked away. Desperate to hide his thoughts he peered through the steamed-up windows, saw Marshal Clarence Fogg emerging from his office. *Doing his rounds*, he thought — *and I was so shocked by King's confession I never did get around to asking him which bank he plans on robbing next . . .*

When he looked back at Cath, she was watching him, her expression quizzical.

'What?'

'Before you looked away I thought I saw something in your eyes. So what do you think? You've been to the mine, you nearly died there. Do you think there's any gold?'

'We both need sleep,' Johnny Dark said evasively. 'Then there's a decision to be made.'

He pushed back his chair, drew Cath's away from the table for her as she stood up, then followed her out into the street. A soft, warm wind was blowing. The moon was high and thin, a sliver of brightness floating in inky skies above the glow of Del Rio's street lamps.

'We found him, didn't we?' Cath said. 'Is that it? Is that what's bothering you?'

'It's making my head spin,' Dark said. 'We found him on the very first day, much too fast, and until my mind catches up with that reality I just don't know what to do next.'

* * *

They slept late the next day, and the question of what they should do now that they had found Nathan King was still unanswered when Dark clattered down the gunbelt stairs at around ten o'clock and stepped out onto the plank walk.

He was thick-headed from sleep, unshaven, hungry, but most of all he was looking for fresh air to clear away the cobwebs so that he could think straight.

What he found was an unexpected, explosive situation that changed everything and almost ended his life.

* * *

The town of Del Rio was quiet. It was the lull between the early morning rush when riders and heavily laden wagons hit town and business premises opened, and the second spell of feverish activity that came before the midday break that usually lasted until the cooler hours of late afternoon.

Knowing that Cath was not yet out of bed, Dark stretched, yawned and walked to the back of the plank walk to stand close to the walls of the rooming house. There, his back flat against the sun-warmed boards, he again filled his lungs with fresh air and looked idly up and down the street. He could smell the heat of the desert, the faint sharp scent of horses drifting down from the livery barn, the aroma of greasy food issuing from the open door of the café. Across the street, the door to Clarence Fogg's office was closed. There was no sign of life, no horses tied up at the rail.

He's out of town, Dark thought. Collecting fines. Chasing rustlers. Talking turkey with Pascal and Tombs or other shady characters. Maybe he had left a deputy in charge, maybe not. It was a quiet town. Trouble was rare.

Out of the corner of his eye he caught a flash of movement. Without urgency, he glanced to his left. A rider had eased his horse out of the alley alongside the bank. As Dark watched, a second followed, then a third. All three stopped by the hitch rail. Two men dismounted.

Dark thought, without too much interest, that the alley must be a short cut from another part of town. No doubt frequently used. Why go the long way round when the alley would save time?

He was about dismiss the ordinary scene from his mind when the men's actions alerted him, warned him that he'd got it wrong. Instead of tying their horses, the two men on foot handed their horses' reins to the third man. He remained in the saddle. That third man was thick-set and sported a sombrero on which silver conchos glittered.

The two men climbed the steps to the bank. Dark saw their hands go to their throats. They pulled bandannas up

103

to cover their faces.

Déjà vu, he thought in amazement. *It's Waco all over again.*

The two men left the bank's heavy doors wide open. The man holding their horses let his own mount swing around so that he had a clear view up and down the street. As he did so he flicked a glance in Dark's direction.

It was the Mexican, Pablo Pascal!

Then, as Dark was swiftly digesting that startling information, the other two men came tumbling out of the bank. The first man took the steps in a couple of long bounds. Two fat gunnysacks swung from his hands. He heaved one up to the Mexican. With the other swinging weightily from one hand he hauled himself awkwardly onto his horse.

The second man came down the steps backwards. A six-gun glittered in his right hand. As he stepped down off the last step he snapped two fast shots into the bank's dark interior. Then he turned and ran for his horse. The flat-crowned hat slipped from his head. It was caught at his throat by the plaited rawhide chin strap. Thinning white hair lifted like cotton in the faint breeze.

Clarence Fogg's question was answered. The bank at the top of Nathan King's list was right there in Del Rio — but Fogg, the town marshal, was nowhere to be seen.

With a muttered curse Dark pounded across the plank walk and jumped down into the dust. The three men were already wheeling their horses away from the bank. Dark saw their spurs flash, saw blood glistening red on sharp rowels. The three horses bounded forward. They came surging away from the bank. Long raking strides carried them down the slope towards Dark in a relentless rush.

Dark drew his pistol. He fired a shot in the air. Still they came on. The bandanna had slipped down from Nathan King's face. His teeth flashed white as he grinned savagely.

One man against three, Dark thought.

I cannot stop them.

Time seemed to stand still. Dark was in the middle of the street. His six-gun was in his hand. The horses were bearing down on him. They were lunging, snorting. So close were they that he imagined he could feel the damp heat of their breath on his face — yet he seemed to have time to watch dispassionately, to think, to plan.

He saw coarse blond hair poking from beneath the third man's stained hat. That man, Rick Tombs, had eased ahead. His wild-eyed horse had moved across the path of the other two.

Calmly, coldly, Dark shot the lean gunslinger's horse from under him.

The big horse went down kicking, sharp hoofs wildly flailing. Tombs thudded heavily on his back in the dust. The gunnysack was torn from his grasp. Blocked by the fallen animal Pascal's horse tried to swerve and lost its footing. It crashed sideways and threw its rider. Roaring his rage, Nathan King stood in his stirrups, hauled on the reins. His horse spun, reared, then jinked sideways to stand quivering close to the far plank walk and facing up the street.

Dark backed away, looked about him. Women were turning to run, holding their skirts. Shop doors were slamming shut. A wagon had stopped, slewed across the street and the driver was standing to flick his whip across the backs of the mules. Men were standing watching the three bank robbers — but nobody was coming forward to help Dark.

Then a shot rang out. Dark, now close to the plank walk, grimaced as pain knifed across his ribs. He spun to face the confusion of struggling horses and men.

Pascal was up on his knees in the dust. His fat face was glistening. He held a pistol in his hand. Smoke trickled from the muzzle. Dark gritted his teeth and swung his pistol to bear on the Mexican. Pascal's six-gun belched flame. The bullet whined past

Dark's ear. Dark pulled back the hammer, fired. Dust puffed between the Mexican's knees. Dark shifted his aim, again pulled the trigger.

A dimple appeared in Pascal's grubby shirt. Suddenly the dimple was wet and red. The Mexican's thick lips fell open. He fired another shot. The bullet thudded harmlessly into the dust. Then he fell sideways and lay still.

Suddenly light-headed, Dark sat down on the edge of the plank walk.

Through the waves of mist obscuring his vision he saw Tombs trying to get Pascal's horse back on its feet. The gunslinger's own horse was dead. But Pascal's horse had broken its leg in the fall. As he realized this the lean gunslinger's curses rang out. He looked across at Dark and his six-gun leaped into his fist. He fired once, twice. Splinters flew from the sidewalk, from the upright.

As if in a dream Dark saw that Tombs's right arm was crooked. Broken by Dark's shot five years ago, it must have been badly set. That disability was affecting his aim.

Tombs fired again. Again the shot missed.

Dark shook his head. The mist cleared. He felt a surge of strength. He snapped a fast shot at Tombs. The gunslinger's hat flew from his head. He snarled, returned the fire. The shot was wild. His face a mask of hate he spun away, ran to recover the gunnysack.

Close to the far plank walk, Nathan King was struggling with his terrified mount. As Dark watched he managed to turn it. The man's sweeping glance took in the chaos, the pandemonium. He urged his mount forward, leaned down far out of the saddle and scooped the Mexican's gunnysack up out of the dust. Tombs was running towards him. King, now moving fast down the street, held out a crooked arm. Tombs leaped forward, grasped it, and swung himself up behind King.

With a shrill yell of triumph, Nathan

King rode at a gallop away from the bank, away from Dark. He swerved around the marooned wagon, then moved his mount back into the middle of the street so that wagon and mules were between him and Dark.

The uninterrupted rattle of hoofs, fading into silence, told Johnny Dark that King and Tombs had made it out of town. Then, feeling the warm blood trickling down his ribs, he closed his eyes and leaned heavily against the timber upright.

11

'You never did tell me what you intended to do about King if you found out he'd left you to die,' Clarence Fogg said.

'I've been racking my brains,' Dark said. 'I still haven't come up with an answer that'd make — '

He broke off with a groan, clamping his teeth shut as the plump, bald doctor jerked a thread tight, knotted it, then pulled down Dark's bloodstained shirt.

'All done. You'll live to pay my bill.'

They were in Fogg's office. The marshal was sprawled in the swivel chair behind his desk, smoke curling from the cigar in his big fist. Dark was sitting stiffly in a straight chair by the window with the warm sun on his back. Cath was in a similar chair in front of the desk, her face pale. A lanky deputy called Spence was leaning against the wall near the rack of gleaming rifles and shotguns.

The shiny-suited doctor, sweating profusely, now snapped shut his black bag, nodded to the marshal and went out onto the sunlit street.

'An answer that'd what?' Fogg said as the door closed.

'Make sense,' Cath said. 'None would make sense before we came to Del Rio, and certainly nothing I can come up with would make sense now.'

Fogg's eyebrows lifted. 'Why now? Because King robbed a bank? That's no surprise. Your husband knew he'd already spent five years in the pen for that same crime.'

'A long time ago I was a young kid, King was a middle-aged liar and I was taken in by him,' Dark said. 'Ever since then I've sworn it wouldn't happen again and, as far as I know, King hasn't changed his ways.' He looked at Fogg. 'Yesterday that man told me his real name is Thomas Dark. What do I do — believe him?'

Fogg gaped. 'What, you reckon King — or Dark — is hinting he's your *father*?'

Dark nodded. 'Not hinting. He told me straight.'

The graze across his ribs was still on fire. The smell of medication was making him feel queasy.

'Once a liar, always a liar,' Deputy Spence said, heading for the door. 'Only sure thing about Nathan King is he robs banks.'

Again the door slammed shut. Fogg sighed.

'He's off out to see what he can dig up. I'm no great believer in posses, but those damn thieves have got to be caught. I could send Spence after them with a couple of men — if he can find anyone willing to ride — or maybe I should go myself . . . '

He shrugged, mashed out the cigar, stared broodingly at the ashes for a moment.

'I'll drink to Spence's last remark about liars,' he said at last, looking across at Dark, 'but even a genuine born liar has to tell the truth at some time in his life — even if it's only when he's ordering his breakfast.'

'I don't think he is telling the truth,' Cath said. 'I can't see any resemblance between John and that man.'

Dark shook his head. 'I take after my ma — '

'Maybe. But that's not enough. There's always something to link a person to both parents: the shape of the ears, the nose, the line of the jaw, the way they move or stand — but there's nothing in your face, or in anything you do.'

Fogg was rocking slowly, his eyes thoughtful.

'You've been without a pa for long enough now to be used to the idea. And, like Spence said, once a liar . . .' He looked speculatively at Dark. 'King's on the run. He'll take some catching. You going to pursue your business with him, or drop everything and ride for home? Leave questions unanswered, because they really ain't worth the bother of chasing a bank robber halfway across Texas?'

Dark hesitated. He could feel Cath's eyes on him, and he knew she would go along with whatever he decided. And he knew that going home was not an option.

'We're going to hang around for a couple of days. Do a lot of serious thinking, then make some hard decisions.'

Fogg grinned happily. 'When you've done your thinking, I know exactly the conclusions you'll come to. You'll go after Nathan King.'

'There's something else,' Dark said, and saw Cath frown. 'I've got unfinished business in Mexico.'

'Well now,' Fogg said softly, 'and here was me thinking you'd forgotten all about that gold mine.'

'It's not just the mine,' Dark said. 'Maybe the mine doesn't even figure in this. But the posse caught King in Pueblo Pequeño, and I'm guessing he went there because he knows the town. One way of getting to the truth is by talking to someone who knows King. The Mexican village he fled to could be a good place to start.'

Clarence Fogg was listening to Dark, but watching Cath.

'I think your wife,' he said, 'is one step ahead of both of us.'

Cath nodded agreement. 'Nathan King is playing all kinds of devious games with you, John,' she said. Her eyes were troubled. 'You never mentioned it, but — did you tell him you'd been a lawman?'

'I made a point of it. Told him we were on opposite sides. He laughed at that, told me there was a damn good reason why I'd never arrest him.'

'He laughed because he had been planning to rob the bank in Del Rio, and then something completely unexpected happened.'

She waited. Dark said nothing.

Fogg said, 'Yeah, you two rode into town.'

'That's right,' Cath said. 'And so it was all coming together for Nathan King. You'd been out of his mind for years, John. In the last year of his term in the state pen he was fully occupied planning the Del Rio bank raid. But suddenly, there you were.'

'And you were making it easy for him,' Fogg said. 'Ordinarily, a good citizen leaves it to the lawmen to chase the bank robbers. But now here you are settin' in front of King telling the man you are the law. And as if that wasn't enough, to make damn sure you'll take a keen interest in everything he does — he tells you he's your pa.'

'You may be right — but why does he want me to go after him?'

'Because he wants you dead,' Fogg said. 'Deep down, you know that — but you just don't know why. So you *will* go after him — '

'I didn't say that — '

'But you will,' Fogg said. 'And when you do, you'll be wearing a badge that says you're my deputy.'

Dark drew a shaky breath.

'No. I intend to go to Pueblo Pequeño, and I intend to ask those questions.'

'Right,' Fogg said. 'But if you look at your wife right now you'll see she's thinking exactly what I'm thinking. King knows you'll go to that Mex village — and when you get there, he'll be waiting.'

'We'll see.'

'More than that, you'll see I'm *right*,' Fogg said.

He hauled his long frame out of the swivel chair, took a bunch of keys off a peg and unlocked the gun rack. His big fingers hovered. Then he selected a Remington shotgun, turned and tossed it all the way across the room to Dark.

'One more thing,' he said. 'King knows you're a lawman, and he's told you he's your pa. But the one thing he's got going for him that's potentially more valuable to his cause than either of those is the young woman sitting right there in front of my desk. It's going to be tough out there, Dark. If your wife rides with you you'll always be vulnerable, always at a disadvantage.'

12

With a few essential supplies in their saddle-bags they chose to leave Del Rio that same day, preferring to put a good part of the long ride behind them by nightfall rather than spend a night in town wasting time.

There was never any question of leaving Cath behind. Dark had expressed his admiration for her courage and skill with a pistol long before they left Laredo for the long ride north. Nothing had happened to change his opinion. And he did not agree with Marshal Clarence Fogg. Far from leaving him vulnerable and at a disadvantage, by riding at his side his capable young wife made him feel stronger and more confident.

They crossed the river in mid-afternoon and pushed on through Ciudad Acuna. Cath, knowing that this was where Rick Tombs spent most of his time, suggested that here the surviving gunslinger and King might have gone to ground. Dark argued otherwise. He knew that King and Tombs would have found a fresh horse for the blond gunslinger then worked hard to put as many miles as possible between themselves and Del Rio. That kind of distance, which ideally would also take them well outside Marshal Fogg's jurisdiction, meant crossing the border and pushing on into Mexico.

Following that theory to its logical conclusion, Dark found himself agreeing with Marshal Fogg: for some reason King was being drawn back to the village of Pueblo Pequeño. Well, that made two of them Dark thought with a wry, inward smile. Two men making for the same small Mexican village for very different reasons — or was that a naïve simplification?

Five years ago he and King had followed this same trail. The ride had culminated in betrayal and violence that had still not been explained. Was King now deliberately drawing the man he had named as his son to some kind of grim termination, using a bank robbery and Dark's badge of office to ensure that Dark hunted him down?

Yet even if he had by accident hit upon the truth, Dark knew that it did him very little good. And in any case, thinking too deeply could create complications where there was none. He and King were riding hard for Pueblo Pequeño. Whatever their reasons, whatever outcome was on the cards, it would be enacted there in that Mexican village.

With his mind as settled as it would ever be, Dark spoke to Cath about his conclusions and they quickly put Ciudad Acuna behind them. Despite the nagging pain from his wound they rode hard throughout the long hot afternoon. By nightfall they had covered almost fifty miles.

That first night was spent in a grove of trees on the banks of a dried-up river-bed that Dark recognized: five years earlier he had camped in the same place with Nathan King. In another eerie echoing of a past experience, he and Cath slept well and were in the saddle before daybreak.

But this time the realization that they were being followed came to Dark not at noon, but when the first light of a new day was brightening the eastern skies. Against that dazzling band of light low down on the horizon, the plume of dust was like the smoke rising from a distant fire. Yet, clear and unmistakable though it was, Dark could not decide if it was being kicked up by one rider, or by several.

As they reined in alongside a grove of cedars and he gave Cath the bad news there was a glint of excitement in her blue eyes.

'Do you think it's them?'

'King and Tombs? If it is, they must have waited for us in Ciudad Acuna and watched us ride through. But can you see bank robbers carrying sacks of stolen money taking that risk?'

'No, and we'd already decided that they'd pushed on to Pueblo Pequeño. But who else can it be. Why would anyone else follow us?'

'I agree. I *know* of nobody else. It has to be them, so what I want you to do is ride — '

'You know two guns are better than one. For that reason, I should stay here with you.'

Dark smiled. 'Cunning can work better than brute force. They know there are two of us, so if they find me here alone they'll be nervous as kittens. They also know I'm fast enough to let them draw first and still beat both of them and, as they look about them, they'll see a score of places that could be hiding a skilled rifleman. Faced by a known gunfighter, and a hidden sharp-shooter, they'll feel like sitting ducks.'

'Then let me do that. Let me hide in those trees with my rifle.'

He shook his head firmly. 'The idea that you *might* be there will be enough to scare them off. So I want you to ride on for a mile, then pull off the trail and wait for me.'

'You could be wrong about beating them to the draw,' Cath said. 'If it comes to shooting, your wound will slow you down.'

'It was Pascal's shot that sliced across my ribs, but he's dead. Tombs was down in the dust, King was fighting his horse. They don't know I was hit.'

'But if the worst comes to the worst — '

'If it does, I want you out of the way — and those riders are getting closer.'

Cath spread her hands helplessly. She rode close, held the horn as she leaned across, touched Dark's cheek with her fingertips and kissed him on the lips.

Then she wheeled her mount, tapped its flanks lightly with her heels and raced off down the trail.

Dark watched her until she rounded a curve that took her out of sight behind the cedars, then moved off the trail and into the trees.

There he dismounted, tied his horse where it couldn't be seen, then found a vantage point behind a fallen tree that gave him a clear view of the trail while affording cover solid enough to stop a cannon ball.

He settled down to wait.

★ ★ ★

Dark had calculated that the men riding in pursuit were no more than fifteen minutes behind them and closing fast. But as he waited, that fifteen minutes dragged slowly to twenty, then thirty — and the day was warming up.

Insects were out in force, and Dark was soon roundly cursing as he slapped at mosquitoes and flies while the sweat trickled down his back and sides and began to soak into the bandages covering his wound. The salt stung like acid. He was hot, sticky, being eaten alive by blood-sucking insects and gritting his teeth against the increasing pain. And so he was flapping his hat at his buzzing tormentors, hugging his side and snatching quick glances at the trail when he heard a loud, metallic click behind him — and went absolutely still.

'All right,' he said despairingly. 'You've caught me cold, so step out of the bushes and let's see your face.'

'I can't believe how easy it was,' Marshal Clarence Fogg said. Branches crackled underfoot as he emerged to join Dark behind the log.

He eased down the six-gun's hammer and grinned. 'Who're you hiding from?'

'Yeah, you're a real joker, Fogg,' Dark said. His heart was pounding. The sweat on his face was as cold as ice. 'You realize I died a thousand deaths when you cocked that thing?'

'Death would have been a real possibility if it'd been anyone else.' Fogg looked around. 'Where's Cath?'

'Waiting up ahead. I got her out of the way when I realized we were being followed.'

'Considering the mess you made of this it might be wiser next time to keep her with you.' Fogg sat on the log, his back to the trail, his eyes thoughtful. 'I asked questions on the way through Acuna. King and Tombs stopped for a horse for Tombs, and bought supplies before heading west. I don't know how long that took. It still puts them ahead of you, but maybe not too far — and whichever way you look at it, Cath's caught in the middle.'

Dark shot him a glance. 'I've seen no sign of them, and we've been crossing a lot of open ground. There's not much cover. If they are too close, Cath will see them and back off.'

'Yeah — just the way you saw me,' Fogg pointed out.

And now Dark was worried. 'Could be I'm under-estimating the opposition — and too much of this is guesswork. I figured the showdown would come in that Mex village, but King could have other ideas. If I can plan an ambush, so can he — and I've told Cath to push on for a full mile. That's a lot of distance between us.' He sprang to his feet. 'Where's your horse?'

'In the trees.'

'Get it,' Dark said, 'then catch me up.'

Swiftly he untied the big white mare, climbed stiffly into the saddle and pulled out onto the trail. He urged the horse to a gallop. A mile, he had said — but how far had Cath ridden? She could have pulled off the trail much sooner — or decided to push on. If she was safe, if nothing had happened, she should hear him coming. If she heard him, she'd step out, wave him down . . .

As Dark rode on, his eyes sweeping from one side of the trail to another, he was bracing himself for the sound of gunfire. If confronted, Cath would fight like a cornered cougar. She had a small Remington pistol, and a Winchester rifle. At the first sign of danger she would draw that pistol and fire a couple of shots. They might be shots aimed at King or Tombs, or shots fired into the air to attract Dark's attention as she wheeled her horse out of danger and prepared to flee. Whatever their purpose, Dark would hear the crack of those shots on the still air.

But so far, he had heard not a sound.

That was reassuring and, as his horse flew down the trail, Dark's gaze was fixed on the tracks he could see in the ground flowing beneath his horse's hoofs. Those tracks were as clear to Dark as the spoor of a wild beast was to a seasoned hunter. They were tracks made by Cath's horse and with those to guide him he felt closer to his wife; felt, in his heart, that nothing could go wrong.

In that manner, following the trail reluctantly laid by a young woman who would have preferred to be with her man, half a mile was rapidly eaten up by the racing horse. Then another swift quarter of a mile passed — and still no menacing or alarming sounds were heard by Dark.

He pounded on, bent low along his

mount's neck, the white mare's hoofs thundering on the hard ground. Now the open country Dark had talked about with Fogg had closed in. The ground was still flat but there were more trees, dark pines pushing in on the trail. Seeing ahead for any distance was impossible. As Dark strained his ears to catch the sound of shots, he heard the drumming of hoofbeats coming up behind him. In one swift backward glance he saw Clarence Fogg, his thin hair flattened, hat raised high and flapping in his right hand as he used it to urge his horse to ever greater speed.

And he was catching Dark.

But now Dark had spotted something a short way ahead.

The trees fell away on his right. Stony ground had prevented growth and a small clearing had been created by nature. Dark had caught sight of a familiar object in the centre of that dusty, treeless area. The sight had sent his spirits plummeting, brought his heart up into his mouth.

With a strange reluctance he slowed the mare. As the horse eased back from a gallop to a canter, to a trot, and then to a walk, Dark noted with dismay the hard ground cut up by the sharp hoofs of milling horses. A keen glance told him that two horses had burst from the ring of trees. He could see where a third horse had been brought to a halt so abrupt it must have dropped back on its haunches. Then there were the unmistakeable signs of chaos, the area where the three horses had come together, their dancing hoofs chopping into the rock-hard earth.

Dark pulled the mare to a stop. He sat there, head hanging, his breathing shallow and painful.

Fogg came up behind him, eased close, his horse blowing hard.

'Whose is the hat?'

'Cath's.'

'Jesus Christ,' Fogg said. Then he leaned across, gripped Dark's arm. 'I heard no shooting, *you* heard no shooting — right?'

'Not a sound.'

'Then she's all right. They've got her — but she's unharmed.'

'What about a gun butt to the head? A knife in the ribs? A man's fist — '

'Cut it out!'

'Goddamn it, she's my *wife* — '

'And you'll get her back. *We'll* get her back.'

Fogg released Dark's arm. He took a moment to control himself, to put a tight rein on his emotions. Then he stretched in the saddle, eased his sore ribs, dismounted, picked up Cath's hat and folded it into his saddle-bag. When he climbed back in the saddle, Fogg was grinning at him.

'It's a set back, Dark. Life's full of 'em. We're all still going in the same direction, all five of us. It's just the groups have been rearranged, two following three instead of the other way around. It'll sort itself out.'

'You like talking, don't you?' Dark said, watching the marshal, marvelling as he realized the old lawman was actually enjoying himself.

'Beats brooding.'

'And riding beats talking. You're right. I don't know what King's playing at, but I know where I can get to the bottom of this mess. The answer lies in Pueblo Pequeño — if not there then in a disused gold mine that nearly cost me my life.'

Fogg's gaze was amused. 'Right, so now who's wasting time talking?'

13

Dusk was closing in on the hill town of Pueblo Pequeño as Dark and Fogg rode in. A steep, narrow street snaked uphill between single-storey adobe houses. Lamplight glowed in the windows. Black-clad women were talking in the open doorway of a general store, pale faces turned towards the approaching riders. Men in baggy, dirty white clothing and floppy sombreros stood or squatted against the wall of a *cantina*. A bell hung still and silent in the open tower of a small church high up the hill, but somewhere a guitar was tinkling and the sweet and haunting melody cast an air of peace and sleepy contentment over the small hill town.

An illusion, Dark thought grimly. If he was right, somewhere in the maze of houses clinging to the hill-side Nathan King and Rick Tombs were lying low.

With a captive. A slim, dark-haired young woman they were cruelly holding hostage.

Looking ahead, he saw several horses tied in front of the *cantina*. They were ragged, ill-fed. King's fine mare was not among them.

'There's the best place to ask questions,' Fogg said, nodding towards the low adobe building. 'And I guess we could both do with a drink.'

Dark grunted. They rode the remaining thirty yards or so, swung down, tied their horses. The lounging Mexicans watched in silence, their black eyes liquid in the fading light. Dark stepped up onto the uneven board gallery. Fogg's boots clumped heavily behind him as he pushed through the greasy blanket hanging across the door.

He'd been aware of the murmur of voices as he approached the *cantina*. Now that murmur was abruptly silenced as half a dozen men turned to stare at the newcomers.

Dark stopped. Fogg pushed in

behind him, stepped to one side with his hand hovering near his six-gun.

It was a room with a low board ceiling. The long bar was a number of thick lengths of wood supported by broken crates. Bottles stood on sagging shelves on the wall behind the bar. A cracked mirror in an ornate gilded frame hung above the bottles. Lanterns scattered about the room bathed room and occupants in smoky yellow light.

Behind the bar a man with a magnificent dark moustache ruined by a jagged knife scar was watching them with suspicion.

No sign, Dark noted, of King or Rick Tombs.

At the end of the crude bar a tall, black-clad man wearing two shiny pistols in ornate tooled holsters was drinking what looked like poor-quality mescal. He had been talking to the scarred man who had now drifted back to him and was leaning against the wall near the shelves. The tall Mexican with the two finely chased six-guns was

137

unshaven but elegant. His dark whiskers added strength to his lean face. He had about him an air of authority. His gaze, as he watched Dark and Fogg cross the room to the bar, was imperious.

Dark ordered beer, sent a coin ringing on the boards. He could smell garlic and greasy food, sour perspiration, unwashed bodies. He guessed that if he walked to the end of the bar and stood close to the gunman he would smell the man's perfume, the pomade he used to groom his glistening black hair. Dark thought he might have to do that. If he was to get sense from anyone, he would be the man to approach.

In a mumbled aside he put the notion to Fogg. The marshal nodded.

'Him, or that barman who looks like he got too close to a sharp knife. Maybe both of 'em. So let's do it.'

Carrying their drinks, they edged down the bar.

Dark addressed the scarred barman.

'We're looking for two men,' he said. 'One's middle-aged, has grey hair, wears a flat black hat. The other's lean, blond, got a crooked right arm.'

The barman shrugged, his eyes blank.

The elegant man with the two guns smiled.

'Mario's English is poor,' he said. 'He understands, but I don't think he can help you. I am Antonio. I have been in town all day. I have not seen those men.'

'There would have been a young woman with them,' Dark said.

Antonio shook his head. 'I am sorry.'

'Look, help me out here. I'm sure they were heading this way, but they could have passed through,' Dark said. 'Could be they were making for a disused gold mine about twenty miles from here.'

Antonio became very still. His eyes darkened. He shot a glance at the scarred barman.

'That mine is disused for a very good

reason,' Antonio said. 'If they value their lives, those men will not go there.'

'Their lives don't have a value,' Fogg said drily. 'They're no-good bank robbers.'

'If the mine is disused,' Dark said, 'why would going there put those men's lives at risk? Is it a dangerous place? Unsafe?'

'Unsafe, yes, because it is a *sacred* place,' Antonio said. 'And, for that reason, of course there is danger there. You see, there is a . . . how do you say, a — '

'*Maldición*,' Mario said. A match flared as he lit the ragged stump of a cigar. 'There is a . . . spell. Men die *como por arte de magia*.'

'Like magic,' Antonio translated. 'There is nothing outwardly wrong with them, but once they have been to that place they do not live for long.'

Fogg looked at Dark.

'You agree with that?'

'I'm here, now. That makes me living proof they're wrong.'

Antonio was frowning.

'Are you saying you have been there, to the mine?'

'I got into some trouble there five years ago.'

'Five years ago!' The Mexican's eyes widened. 'Ah, yes, now I remember, there was a story at the time about a terrible gunfight in which a lot of blood was spilled. Then, on that same night, a man rode down from the hills into Pueblo Pequeño. He was taken by the *rurales* — the federal police — then by lawmen who came riding in from Texas — '

'Same man I'm looking for today,' Dark cut in. 'Nathan King. He'd robbed a bank in Waco, was taken from here to do five years in the pen.'

'And the other man, the man in the mine when the bullets were flying and the blood was flowing — that was you?'

Dark nodded. 'Me, yes — and it was my blood . . .

While they were talking the scar-faced man called Mario had jammed the cigar in the corner of his mouth and walked away. Now he returned, pushing through a curtained doorway that led to a back room. He was holding a small cigar box. He placed it on the bar in front of Dark, took the cigar from his mouth in a shower of sparks and ash and growled at Antonio in rapid Spanish.

The lean man's eyes danced with amusement.

'Mario tells me that if you were spilling your blood at the mine five years ago, then this must be yours.'

'Nope, I've never seen that thing before tonight,' Dark said.

'Yeah, well, I've got me a nasty feeling that I can't quite put a finger on,' Clarence Fogg said, with an uneasy glance at his companion. 'You'd best open it — but before you do, brace yourself for a shock.'

Dark slid the box towards him. The stained and ripped paper label covered the lid and the back of the box, forming a weak hinge. Dark grasped the box.

Took hold of the edge of the small lid. Lifted it open.

And took a deep breath.

Inside the box, on filthy, crumpled tissue paper, there lay three mummified fingers.

'You're right,' he said tightly. 'These were mine a long time ago, but I've got used to being without them.' He looked at Mario, then sideways at Antonio. 'If Mario's got hold of these, someone else must have been into the mine, some of your people. It's either sacred, or it's not — so which is it?'

Antonio spread his hands. 'I am telling you the truth. But of course, there are some here in Pueblo Pequeño who are more foolhardy than others. Youngsters who are not without fear but who will do anything for a dare. At some time they must have plucked up their courage and walked inside that place, just a little way, you understand, just far enough to find these' — he gestured at the gruesome remains — 'but when they stuffed them into their pockets their courage trickled away like water and they ran for their lives.'

'Yeah, I can see youngsters doing that,' Dark said, nodding slowly, thoughtfully. 'And I can see how this sacred business would keep superstitious adults away. There can't be many who know what lies deeper inside that mine.'

'Deeply *religious* adults,' Antonio said softly.

Suddenly there was a heavy silence in that smoky *cantina*, and Dark realized that Mario and Antonio were not the only people listening to the conversation. He was aware that the other drinkers, at the bar and sitting at tables deep in the shadows, had moved closer. A glance about him told him that while some of the men pressing closer were simple peasants, others were more menacing. He saw dark sombreros and the swarthy, evil faces of mountain bandits, hands hovering near weapons — guns, knives — from lifelong habit, eyes glittering like those of poisonous snakes in the dim lamplight.

'You are right, but please allow me to amend your words,' Antonio said. 'The truth is that there are not many *who are still alive and well and able to tell others what they discovered*,' he stated. He spoke clearly, his eyes sweeping the room, and in those accented tones there was a subtle warning that sent a chill of apprehension rippling through Dark's veins.

He had been about to put before Antonio something that he was convinced would open the man's mind to Dark's plight, make him less reluctant to offer his help and, perhaps, enlist the help of others. The knowledge these people had of the disused mine had been passed from mouth to mouth over the years. That knowledge was sparse, and flawed: they knew the shabby hole in the hillside with its crumbling roof and broken timber props was sacred — but little more. And Dark guessed that was because at some time in the past a wise man of the town had created and spread a dark rumour to guarantee that if the mine had hidden secrets, those secrets would remain buried.

The mine did hold secrets. King's lies had forced a younger and more gullible Dark into a brief but painful sojourn in that dismal place, but it had been the withering fire from another man's gun that had driven him deeper underground. His left hand dripping blood, he had been searching desperately for a way out. He had found that — and much more.

But the atmosphere in the *cantina* had changed. Talk of the mine had been overheard. Those close to Dark and Fogg had seen the grubby cigar box, its sinister contents. To reveal to these superstitious men, now, what he had stumbled across on his bloody struggle through the bowels of the earth, was a risk he could not take.

If he was to find Cath, there had to be another way.

Dark closed the cigar-box with a snap, looked at Antonio and forced a smile.

'You've treated me with politeness when I have intruded on your past, and your beliefs. Thank you. It's time we went and left you in peace.'

'Went where, Mr . . . ?

'John Dark, of Laredo. And this is Clarence Fogg, of Del Rio.'

Antonio dipped his head. 'So, I ask again — where are you going?'

'To find my wife,' Dark said. 'That shouldn't take me anywhere near your mine.'

Antonio's eyes flickered.

'Go in peace,' he said quietly, and a flash of his black eyes silenced the sudden murmur of discontent that rippled around the smoky room.

Outside in the cooling night air, as they stood for a moment on the rickety gallery, Fogg let his breath go explosively.

'You didn't mention we were lawmen.'

'Something in reserve,' Dark said.

'Could come in useful when we need it.'

'No time like now. There was a lot of bad feeling in there, too many weapons for my delicate nerves,' Fogg said feelingly. 'But I'll ask the same question that feller Antonio put to you: where are we going? Back on the trail you admitted you don't know what King's up to. You reckoned the answer lies here in Pueblo Pequeño — or in that goddamn mine I'm sick of hearing about. OK, we've asked in the town. So now what? Because after what we heard in there that mine is sure as hell out of bounds.'

'Maybe.'

'No maybe about it,' Fogg said forcefully.

Dark listened to the murmur of voices from the *cantina*, and noted that the volume had increased.

'They're getting riled in there,' he said, 'so the safest place for us is out there in the woods with a fire burning, coffee brewing, and food sizzling in my

148

blackened skillet.'

'And then . . . ?'

'And then when we've eaten,' Dark said, 'I'll show you something that could change your mind about that mine, and Antonio's decision not to help me.'

14

Dark and Fogg rode north-west out of Pueblo Pequeño, the last glimmers of daylight streaking the skies behind them as they urged their horses off the trail and worked them up through the woods blanketing the foothills of the Sierra del Carmen. They were riding across the slope at an angle that took them gently uphill on a carpet of dry, crackling leaves and twigs. And, as he rode a few yards ahead of the Del Rio marshal, Dark was mentally ticking off the miles.

After a little less than an hour, he called a halt.

'We're halfway between the town and the mine,' he said, swinging down from the saddle.

Fogg, still sitting on his horse with his hands folded on the horn, was regarding him with disbelief.

'After what happened back there, you took us *towards* that creepy place?'

'The other direction takes us deeper into Mexico. I can't see King going that way.'

'Yeah, well, this way is just *guaranteed* to make those Mexicans suspicious. Christ, even now a bunch of them could be on our tail — '

'You're worrying too much — '

'That's because you're treading in deep waters, and that's asking for trouble, Dark.'

'What I'm doing,' Dark said, 'is heating the pot to get something to boil over. The reaction could come from those fellers back at the *cantina*, or from Nathan King. Either way is welcome if it gets Cath back, so we'll see . . .'

Fogg swore softly as he swung down. 'I just hope what you've got to show me saves us from getting carved up by bloodthirsty bandits with long knives.'

And while tying his horse and loosening the cinch he cast several worried glances towards the dark encroaching trees.

By the time they had eaten their fill it was full dark, and a thin moon was floating in clear skies. As Fogg settled back by the fire with a tin cup of coffee and rolled a cigarette, Dark walked off a little way and dug into his saddle-bag. When he returned to the fire he was carrying a soft leather pouch. He hunkered down on the other side of the fire and hefted the supple little poke, reflectively his eyes distant.

'I thought I was a goner,' he said, 'when that slug tore off my fingers. I was in agony, bleeding like a stuck pig, deafened by a hail of bullets. So what I did was what any man would have done — I turned into the tunnel and ran for my life. It was cold, pitch dark, and I was scrambling downhill and scraping most of my skin off as I bounced off the walls. As far as I knew the tunnel went so far, then stopped. When I ran into something solid that tore my shin and brought me crashing full length, I thought it was the end. I struck a match, held it high. Rocks had tumbled down. I was sprawled across them — but on my right there was a jagged vertical fissure in the wall. It looked like a fresh scar. I could imagine an earth tremor fracturing those solid stone walls, or Mexicans with picks and shovels giving up and walking away from the old workings, not realizing the damage they'd caused.'

Dark grinned at Fogg.

'I didn't care, didn't waste time thinking about the whys and wherefores. I shot through that crack like a rabbit down a hole. The passage was narrow, dark, I was running blind, running for my life. Then, after what seemed like hours, the rocky floor began sloping upwards and I could feel the fresh night air on my face. The tunnel levelled out. There was an opening, ahead of me and above. The moon was shining through, a shaft of pure white light. A stroke of luck. Because at that place a deep gully like a dry water course cut across the passage. Six feet deep. If I'd fallen into that I'd've broken my neck. But, like I said, the moon was shining — and that was when I got the second stroke of luck. The moon was in just the right position. Its slanting light not only saved me from that gully, it struck the wall of the passage just before that dangerous dry wash. Where it struck, something glittered.'

'Jesus H. Christ!' Fogg said.

'I used the butt of my six-gun to chip away at that seam,' Dark said, 'then clawed my way out of the earth and flopped down on the steep hillside listening to the raised voices of men arguing in the clearing far below . . . then, after a while, the sound of horses . . . and then blessed silence.'

Dark tossed the leather pouch to Fogg. The lawman loosened the drawstring, tipped the small but heavy chunk of rock into his palm. He leaned forward, held the stone close to the fire, let the flickering flames glint on the fine veins of yellow gold.

He looked up at Dark.

'Is this what's going to change my mind?'

'I'm thinking more of Antonio.'

'Yeah.' Fogg pursed his lips. 'Something like this could make that man think twice about superstition.'

'Something like this,' Dark said, 'could cost us our lives — so we take care, think it through.'

Fogg flicked his cigarette into the fire, drained the last of his coffee and put down his cup. As he did so he turned to flick a glance towards the woods, then looked towards Dark.

'You hear that?'

'I heard something.'

'Right. So keep listening, because I've got me another of those feelings . . .'

He shook his head, found a stick, poked at the glowing embers while watching Dark intently.

'Anything strike you about the way Antonio gave us the bad news?'

'About few men visiting the mine and living to tell the tale?' Dark nodded. 'I don't know about you, but I got the feeling he wasn't talking to us.'

'Damn right. He was talking real loud, making sure *everyone* in that room got the message.' Fogg's eyes were glinting. 'So you tell me, why would a man do that?'

Suddenly Dark realized where Fogg, the wily old marshal, was leading him. He took a deep breath, absently rubbed his sore ribs.

'If you're suggesting Antonio knows about the gold — I think you're wrong. If he knows, he'd've done something about it long before now.'

'Not if he stumbled on it recently. Not if he's fighting to keep it a secret while he works on the puzzle of how to get it out of there without anyone knowing.' He cocked his head at Dark. 'Or maybe you've come up with another good reason for him keeping folk away from that place — outside of gold, or superstition.'

156

'I haven't. But I'm absolutely convinced he does not know about the gold,' Dark said, 'and that makes the little chunk of rock I stumbled on five years ago a mighty powerful weapon.'

* * *

The fire was a soft, dying glow. Close by it but under cover of the trees, Dark lay restlessly in his blankets with his hands laced behind his head. He could see Fogg, ten yards away. The marshal appeared to be asleep, hat tipped over his eyes, though less than ten minutes had passed since they stopped talking and settled down for the night.

For Dark, sleep was impossible.

He was accustomed to the myriad clicks and snaps and muted cries of a forest by night, but unaccountably those familiar sounds were making him nervous. He guessed that this was because his thoughts were with Cath. Three years of marriage had brought them very close. He could imagine her torment, knew what she must be thinking, knew that she would expect him to find her, release her — yet he had no idea how to go about it.

The one hope he could see lay with Antonio, and Fogg had been all for confronting him that night. He talked with growing optimism of the panic they could cause in the man by threatening to broadcast the mine's secrets. Dark had been less certain. In the end they had agreed to return to Pueblo Pequeño at first light, thus catching the tall Mexican at his lowest ebb and at a considerable disadvantage.

Always supposing, Dark had pointed out, that they got through the night without incident.

So now he lay with his eyes half closed, listening to the gargling whistle of the marshal's snores and tossing up whether to crawl out of his blankets, throw some sticks on the fire and heat up the coffee, or —

His eyes flicked open.

A horse had whickered, not too far away.

Quickly he rolled out of his blankets, reached for his gunbelt. Up on his knees, he strapped it on. Then he crawled across the damp grass to the other man.

'Someone out there,' he whispered, his hand on Fogg's shoulder.

Instantly awake, immediately alert, Fogg rolled onto his back.

'Where?'

Dark shook his head, motioned for silence. He stood up, backed away then melted into the trees. Like a snake, Fogg slid out of his blankets. In one smooth motion he picked up his gunbelt and came to his feet. Then he too slipped into the woods and was gone from sight.

Pistol drawn and cocked, Dark waited.

Again the horse whickered, now much closer. There seemed to be just the one — and he thought that was strange. For a night raid the Mexicans would come in numbers: three or four at the very least, attacking from the front and both flanks.

He heard a soft clicking.

Away to his left Fogg was looking at him through the trees, clicking his tongue to attract Dark's attention, and pointing. He was also holstering his pistol. Frowning, Dark looked where the marshal had indicated. For a moment the different angle and a stand of trees blocked his view, prevented him from seeing anything. Then he saw the horse. It walked slowly out of the trees. In the moonlight the sheen of its black coat was lustrous, the metal of its bridle fittings as bright as fine silver.

And then from the horse, Dark looked at the rider.

It was the man called Antonio.

15

The tall Mexican walked his horse close to the fire and swung out of the saddle. The horse wandered a few yards then stopped, held by the trailing reins. Antonio looked about him.

Dark and Fogg had melted back into the woods. Dark saw the Mexican's eyes follow the line of trees; saw the moonlight glint on the man's slick black hair as he doffed his hat, the faint smile on his lean face as he hunkered down and lazily used a stick to stir the fire's glowing embers.

He was alone, thirty yards away from the edge of the woods, without cover.

He can see our horses so he knows we're somewhere out here, watching him, Dark thought. *Knows both of us could even now have our rifles up at the shoulder; be taking a bead on his well-groomed head. We planned to catch him at dawn, put him at a disadvantage. Instead, he's deliberately ridden into a situation where other men hold all the high cards. Why would he do that?*

The question intrigued Dark. He wondered if the man's visit had anything to do with the gold mine, with the chunk of ore Dark had for five years kept in a soft leather pouch. If it did — in a way that was favourable and perhaps profitable for the Mexican — then this could be a way to Nathan King, and through King to Cath.

As thoughts raced, undirected and unchecked, the answer became more intriguing than the question and therefore irresistible. Dark took a deep breath, and stepped out of the woods.

Antonio looked up, watched him begin to walk towards the fire; glanced to his right as Fogg took his cue from Dark and also stepped into the moonlight. When both men were halfway between woods and fire, Antonio stood up without haste and

162

almost casually snapped his fingers.

Like ghosts materializing through the moon-cast shadows of the woods on either side of Dark and Fogg, armed, white-clad Mexicans slipped silently into the clearing. They clutched a motley selection of rifles and pistols. A startling, metallic rattling filled the clearing as those weapons were cocked.

For show, Dark thought. *They're letting us know what we're up against, how one hasty move will bring sudden, violent death.*

Dark counted four men on either side. Teeth flashed white in swarthy faces under floppy hats as the men closed in, grinning happily. They handled their old weapons as carelessly as they would sticks — and, Dark guessed, they would use them just as carelessly to kill, or maim.

Four of the men formed a tight half circle behind Dark and Fogg. Two of the others moved to their spread blankets and picked up Fogg's Winchester, the Remington shotgun the marshal had given to Dark. The remaining two crossed to the horses and checked the saddles on Fogg's roan, Dark's white mare, tightened the cinches, brought the horses close to the group around the fire.

'And now your gunbelts, please,' Antonio said quietly — and held out a hand.

'I don't see any sign of a badge,' Fogg said, 'and I don't recall hearing an explanation for this nonsense.'

'That will come,' Antonio said.

'Not good enough, not soon enough,' Dark said, and made to step forward.

Instantly a rifle barrel whacked the back of his knee. His leg folded. He lurched sideways. A sweaty arm encircled his neck, holding him up, cutting off his breath. A hard gun muzzle was rammed into his back.

'For me, this is more than good enough,' Antonio said. 'For me, this is the ultimate *perfection*.'

His words were still, in their way, polite — but the kid gloves had been stripped off to expose the hard fists of the man's power. At a curt nod from Antonio, Dark and Fogg were overwhelmed by a swarm of Mexicans. Their arms were seized, wrenched behind their backs. Rough hands stripped them of their gunbelts. Others used rawhide thongs to lash their hands in front of them. Then they were bundled onto their horses.

Antonio watched all of this impassively, without speaking. When Dark and Fogg were settled, bound hands clutching their saddle horns, another nod sent several of the Mexicans into the woods. They returned with horses. The group mounted, prepared to move off.

'Are you going to tell us why?' Fogg said.

'All will become clear,' Antonio said, 'when we reach town. But when that happens, I guarantee you will be sorry you asked.'

★ ★ ★

They rode into the main street of Pueblo Pequeño when the moon had slipped behind swollen clouds and the dust underfoot was spattered with a warm, persistent rain. The street was deserted. On one or two of the adobe dwellings a sputtering lantern hung from an iron bracket, but the main illumination spilled from the saloon, and from another building a short way up the hill.

Outside that second building, Dark saw, there stood several men in uniform.

The group, with its prisoners, rode straight past the saloon. As they passed, Dark snatched a glance through the door from which the greasy blanket was now tied back. The room was almost empty. He could detect nothing out of the ordinary.

Fogg edged his roan closer.

'We're in trouble,' he growled under his breath. 'That's a bunch of *rurales* waiting for us. Something's gone badly wrong.'

The second building was the jail. The walls were thick. Fancy wrought-iron bars covered small windows. The door was solid timber, banded with iron.

Two of the waiting men stepped forward as the riders drew near. They wore hats and tunics, knee-high boots that had once been glossy but were now scuffed and stained with dried mud.

In the doorway a fat, moustachioed officer who wore his uniform jacket unbuttoned and his dirty white shirt open to expose a chest matted with dark hair was smoking a cigar and watching proceedings.

In streams of rapid Spanish the two junior officers shouted orders. The eight-man escort that had brought Dark and Fogg down from the hills was dismissed, and their horses clattered away down the street towards the saloon.

Antonio dismounted and stood with his back to the street, one hand resting theatrically on his pistol. The two officers strutted forward. Still bound,

Dark and Fogg were dragged from their horses and bundled inside the building.

They stumbled up the steps and were taken straight through the office. Beyond, through a wide arched opening, there was a large chamber with high windows and a dirt floor. A table and chairs stood in the centre. The only light came from a lamp standing on the table. The dull flame could barely be seen through the lamp's blackened glass, and its light was not strong enough to illuminate the empty cells lining the three walls.

Dark was pushed and kicked into one cell, Fogg into another. The doors clanged shut. Keys turned. The *rurales* returned to the office.

'And all we can do now,' Clarence Fogg said, 'is sit and wait for the firing squad.'

16

Dark must have dozed.

After Fogg's gloomy pronouncement there had been nothing more to say. He had thrown himself onto the hard cot with its corn-husk mattress and single filthy blanket, and drifted away into a half-world of light and dark, reality and dreams.

He was jerked awake by a harsh scraping that set his teeth on edge. When he started up on the bunk he saw that Antonio was straddling a chair he had dragged close to the two cells occupied by the prisoners. A thin cigar dangled from his cruel lips as he waited for their attention.

Dark swung his feet down and looked through into the adjoining cell. Fogg was already up off his cot and standing holding the bars as he watched Antonio.

The Mexican took the cigar from his lips and flashed a grin.

'So now you know what happens in Pueblo Pequeño,' he said, 'to those who commit a brutal murder.'

'What the hell are you talking about?' Fogg growled.

Antonio's eyebrows lifted.

'You don't remember?' He spread his hands, the thin cigar glowing. 'This evening after talking to me you walked out of the *cantina*. For some reason you went around the back, where Mario was . . . answering a call of nature . . . you understand? Perhaps you talked to him. I don't know, so, no matter.'

He paused, waiting for a reaction, getting none. He shrugged.

'But then for some crazy reason, using an iron bar that was lying in a patch of weeds, one or both of you smashed poor Mario's skull. You left him there, bleeding, dying — and you calmly rode out of Pueblo Pequeño.'

'And the rest we know, or can guess,' Fogg said. 'A trumped up charge.

170

Vigilantes riding into the woods to pounce on unsuspecting innocent men. Those men thrown into a filthy cell — to await what? A rigged trial?'

Antonio grinned. 'For what? Why waste time that is worth money to these simple farmers? There were half-a-dozen witnesses to the killing. If it was possible to look into Mario's dead eyes we would see, frozen there, your frenzied faces as you beat him to death.'

'Why would we commit murder?'

That was Johnny Dark. He had approached the bars and was looking hard at Antonio, trying to see behind the mocking black eyes that were the dominant feature in the man's the lean, unshaven face. Now those eyes switched to Dark.

'Why would we kill Mario?' Dark repeated. 'And, because I know damn well we *didn't* kill him, why are we being framed?'

The air of amused insolence left Antonio. He pursed his lips, stared at his glowing cigar for a few moments, then dropped it to the dirt floor and ground it to shreds of tobacco with his boot.

When he looked at Dark, his eyes were like black stones washed by the icy waters of a winter storm.

'The answer to your question is wrapped in the passage of time,' he said, 'and in the story of what happened before and after dramatic incidents in the life of one man. But it is not my story. For that,' he said, 'you must talk to your visitor.'

The visitor had been listening.

As Dark watched in astonishment, he came through the arched opening that led to the office of the *rurales*. Beneath the black hat with its plaited rawhide band was a familiar face that bore a look of triumph.

Dark's visitor was Nathan King.

* * *

'So this is your doing.'

A flat statement. Asking a question

would have been a waste of time because, in his heart, Dark knew the answer. So he said the words simply to watch the reaction of the man who had called himself Nathan King and Thomas Dark, but in all probability was neither of those.

King was in Clarence Fogg's cell. Fogg had been taken from there by Antonio, at gunpoint. King had dragged Antonio's chair inside, and was sitting close to the bars that separated him from Dark.

So far, keeping a fierce check on his emotions and his tongue, Dark had not mentioned Cath. *Let the other man do that*, he had told himself. *Let the other man make the running*.

'Sure it's my doing,' King said now. 'I've been after you ever since I saw you in Del Rio five years ago and realized you were Emma James's boy. And now, by God, I've got you.'

Ignoring the suppressed fury tightening the man's voice, Dark nodded.

'Yes,' he said, 'James *was* my

mother's name before she married.'

'My *wife's* name,' King said. 'First it was James — and then, in a simple church ceremony, it became Dark.'

Dark shook his head. 'No. I'm older and wiser now, and I can see you for what you are. You're a man who lies because he knows of no other way, and you've just told another. Mister, I look at you and I know for certain you're not my father.'

The trace of a smile curled King's lips.

'All right, I admit it. That was a lie, tossed into the mixture to see what mischief it would work. You're not my son, and for that I thank God.'

'Then that lie makes a lie of the other. If I'm not your son, you cannot be my mother's husband.'

'Tell me one good reason why not,' King said.

Dark had been sitting on the cot as they talked, looking across the cell and through the bars at King. Now he leaped to his feet and crossed to the bars facing the room's open space, grasped them with both hands, closed his eyes and rested his forehead against the cool metal.

He knew that King was watching him, waiting, undoubtedly following with understandable accuracy the trail of Dark's thoughts. Because of course, if he believed King then there was but one conclusion that could be reached: King had been married to Dark's mother, but she had been unfaithful; she had been with another man.

Yet how could that be? In southern Texas they had lived several miles from town, their nearest neighbour five miles distant and he a man of eighty who had been nursing a sick wife. For a woman to be unfaithful there must be the desire, and the opportunity — and Johnny Dark refused to believe the one, and knew without question that in their remote location the other did not exist.

His eyes flicked open as he heard the scrape of a match, the soft hiss of the flame. When he turned his head he saw

King blowing smoke, his eyes knowing and amused.

'Remember what Rick Tombs said in Del Rio, out there in the hot sun with Pablo Pascal back in the saloon with his head cracked wide open?'

'Tombs said a lot to me,' Dark said. 'Most of it was rubbish.'

'Yeah, well, what I'd particularly like you to remember is him reminding you that when you shave, you use a piece of glass, a cracked mirror. How every morning when you look into that cracked mirror, you see the answer to your question.'

King sucked on his cigarette, let the smoke out through his nostrils, narrowed his eyes, jabbed a finger towards Dark.

'What any young kid wants to see when he looks in a mirror is him growing to look like his pa. He wants to see the image of his pa. And what you see looking back at you, then and now,' King said softly, 'is the image of an Indian.'

Dark went cold. His mind raced, looking back at a thousand images, recalling a thousand memories, feeling again a thousand insults. His scalp prickled. He felt the ridge of the cot behind his knees, and sat down hard.

'Go on,' he said huskily. 'If you've got more lies tell them, get it over with.'

'It's past the time for lies,' King said. 'The truth is your ma was taken by the Comanche. When the army got her back from the hell of the Staked Plains, she was pregnant. I lasted two years after the baby came — you came, after you were born. What else could I do? I loved that woman, always had and deep down always will. But a white woman taken by Indians is soiled goods, John, and I couldn't stand the looks of the townsfolk, the silences . . . and, Christ, worst of all I couldn't stand to look at *you* because every time I looked at you I was reminded of that damned redskin, of what he had done, of what had happened out there to my wife, the woman I worshipped.'

'And some twenty years later,' Dark said, 'I walked into a saloon in Del Rio and, just like that, you decided to kill me.'

'That day made it possible, but the decision had been made years ago. I'd soon come to realize that riding away from my wife and my home and a skinny little 'breed kid did nothing to purge my demons.'

'So why not in Del Rio on that first day? Or did you try? Did Pascal and Tombs make their play under orders from you?'

'That was *your* play. They fell foul of a kid with an itchy trigger finger who didn't know how to back off.'

Dark nodded, remembering. 'I was like that, then — Christ, I *was* a kid, I was still growing up.' He shook his head, still puzzled. 'But why drag me across the desert? Why leave me to die in that crumbling gold mine?'

King laughed. He stood up, kicked the chair across the cell and walked to the door.

'Poetic justice, son.'

He stopped as the last word left his lips, and Dark could have sworn he saw the eyes recoil, a spasm of pain cross the older man's face. Then the moment had passed.

'Poetic justice,' Nathan King repeated softly. 'That gold mine ruined me, because long after I left your ma I joined forces with Antonio and we sank money into it and discovered there never was any gold. Killing you in that place was . . . a sacrifice to whatever gods have been laughing at me and ruining my life. I wanted them to back off — but even offering you up to them wasn't enough, and it all went wrong.'

He was outside the cell. His hand was on the cold iron bars.

'So now it has to be here. Blindfolded. In front of a Mexican firing squad. Gunned down at dawn for a murder you didn't commit, but in reality making the final payment for a crime that was not yours, nor even your mother's. You're going to pay for a crime committed twenty-six years ago by an unknown Comanche.'

King let go of the bars and stepped away and now there was a smile on his face, a smile that was at once gleeful, and evil.

'And you know what? When you get marched out in front of that firing squad, that's when poetic justice really reaches fulfilment,' he said. 'Because when you're staring into those rifle muzzles — yeah, I know you're tough enough to refuse the blindfold — the big thing burning into your mind won't be pain, nor even the death that's staring you in the face, but the knowledge that somewhere out there, old Thomas Dark has got hold of your purty little wife.'

And with a broad wink at Dark, Nathan King turned and stalked out of the room.

17

'Did you ask about Cath?'

Fogg was back in his cell. The rain was beating on the roof of the jail, dripping through holes and spattering the dirt floor, splashing on the table and hissing on the lamp's hot glass chimney.

Dark guessed it was well past midnight. And for the past few minutes he had been listening to the street door opening and closing, the sounds of men leaving.

'King's a liar, so I didn't waste my breath. Didn't need to. I waited, and in the end he told me,' he said.

'It's Dark now, isn't it, not King?' Fogg said. 'He was married to your mother. That, at least, turned out to be true.'

Dark had quickly run through King's story for the Del Rio marshal, had watched the grey eyes take in his appearance when he mentioned the Comanche, seen the look of surprised realization that was as quickly masked, as quickly shrugged off as unimportant.

'In adult life I knew him first as King, to me that's who he'll always be,' Dark said. 'But names don't matter. He's admitted he's got Cath. Now we think hard, come up with ideas — '

'And execute them fast,' Fogg said. 'The *rurales* are not wasting any time. While I was out there, I was told we're to be taken out back of the jail at dawn.'

'Who? Who told you?'

'The *rurales*' big chief, the pompous fool with the moustache and the hairy chest under unwashed clothes.'

'He out there now?'

'Nope. He went home. So did one of his men. The other one's still there' — King cocked his head, listening — 'drinking coffee, talking to Antonio.'

'Call him. Call Antonio.'

'You worked something out?'

Dark slipped the soft leather pouch

out of his pocket, quickly told the marshal what he intended to do.

Fogg chewed his lip. 'I can't come up with anything better, and it just might work. Hell, it *has* to work — or we're done for.'

'I'm about to make it work. Hold fire. Don't start yelling until I tell you.'

Dark put down the pouch holding the gold nugget and sat on the edge of the cot. He turned sideways, clenched his teeth, hesitated for a second then lifted his arm. Then he reached under his shirt and without pause ripped the dressing from his wound. His lips peeled back from his teeth as agony raked across his skin like red-hot coals. The bandage had been stuck to the dried blood. He could almost hear the stitches pulling loose from skin, the tender flesh parting.

Sucking in one deep breath after another he let his head fall back and, with his eyes clamped shut, pressed his shirt to the now open wound. He waited, felt the hot stickiness soak through the cloth and warm his fingers. Blanked his mind to the sickness that caught at his throat, the weakness that turned muscle to water.

He sat like that for several minutes, listening to his own harsh breathing, until the blood soaking through his shirt was running down the back of the hand holding it in place.

He opened his eyes.

Sitting on the edge of the cot he was at the very limit of the weak light cast by the lamp. Antonio would see him, and Dark would make sure that the blood soaking his shirt caught the weak light enough to glisten and be noticed. But to see clearly what Dark had to offer, Antonio would have to approach Dark, or Dark go to him. That was not going to happen — and now Dark could give weakness and loss of blood as his reason for staying put.

Taking a deep breath, Dark loosened the pouch's drawstring. He worked his behind back across the cot until he was sitting with his back against the bars.

Then he looked across at Fogg, and nodded.

The marshal was watching him. His face was grim.

'Was that necessary?'

'Yes. There was no other way. So call him. And get close up against the bars between these two cells. When he comes in — when *they* come in — act as if your whole attention is on what's going on between me and Antonio.'

Then he licked suddenly dry lips and waited nervously as Fogg filled his lungs and hollered for the tall Mexican.

When Antonio at last answered the marshal's shouting and came through from the office, he was accompanied by the junior officer.

He's no fool, Dark thought, *but by being cautious he's playing into my hands.*

'What do you want?' Antonio said, smirking as he walked up to Dark's cell. 'Are you about to plead for your life, and the life of your friend?' He pulled a silver watch out of his pocket, snapped it open. 'I can tell you now, you are wasting time — and the time you have left is just a little under six hours.'

The watch closed with a snap.

Dark said, 'I don't want anything. You want something, Antonio, and what I'm about to show you will change your life.'

He held up his hand. The leather pouch was balanced on the palm of his hand.

Antonio stared. But he was not looking at the pouch. He'd noticed the blood.

'What is that? What is this nonsense?'

'Nonsense?' Dark forced a chuckle, let weakness creep into his voice. 'I was wounded in Del Rio, shot by a countryman of yours called Pablo Pascal. The wound reopened when I was thrown into this cell. But forget my troubles, concentrate on this, on your future prosperity.'

Again he lifted the pouch.

'You know I was in your mine five years ago, that there was a gunfight in which I lost three of my fingers. But you also know I got out — when two men were guarding the entrance. And what I have here — '

'I am already ahead of you, already disbelieving.' Antonio snorted his contempt, slipped the silver watch into his pocket, made to turn away. 'It is now *my* time you are wasting. There is no gold in that filthy, useless mine — '

'If I got out when armed men were guarding the only entrance,' Dark said, 'then I must have found another way. If I found another way, then isn't it also possible that in a tunnel never before seen by man I stumbled across a rich vein of gold?'

Antonio had stopped. He turned back to the cell. Dark could almost see his mind working, the sudden greed shining in the black eyes.

'Let me see.'

'Get your man to turn the key, open the door.'

Antonio laughed. 'Do you think I am a loco? To open the door for you now would be *muy tonto* — '

'I'm finding it difficult to move. If you're worried, bring the constable in with you. What can go wrong? Nothing. There's two of you, I'm weak, I've lost a lot of blood . . . '

Antonio silenced him with an imperious flap of the hand. As Dark watched he hesitated, stroking his chin. His eyes, narrowed in thought, were darting here and there as if seeking help with a problem. Then he straightened to his full height and snapped a command. At once the constable stepped forward, keys jingling, and opened the cell door. Antonio stepped inside.

Dark held his breath. A wise man, a man thinking clearly, would tell the constable to stay outside and lock the door. But he knew Antonio was not thinking clearly. The tall Mexican's heart was pounding. His thoughts were galloping out of control. He had eyes only for the soft leather pouch in Dark's hand.

Unable to disguise his eagerness he

walked across the cell, drew close to the injured prisoner. The constable followed. He, too, was not using his head. It was late, he was tired. His colleagues had finished for the day and would be enjoying a drink in the smoky atmosphere of the saloon, or heading home. His mind with them instead of with his duties, he walked blindly after Antonio.

Behind him, the cell door gaped open.

Dark had already moved awkwardly across the cot to meet Antonio. He swung his feet to the floor and held out the pouch. Antonio reached for it. His fingers were inches away —

Dark let the pouch fall. His right hand whipped across and lifted Antonio's six-gun from its holster. In a continuation of the same rapid, blurred movement he brought the pistol around in a wide swing and slammed the barrel across the Mexican's head.

The tall man's eyes rolled. His knees buckled.

Even as Antonio went down, Dark

saw Fogg move. The *rurales* constable had strayed too close to the bars. Fogg's arm snaked through, looped around the man's throat. The man's hat fell off. His head cracked against the bars. Fogg braced his free hand against the bars and tightened his grip. The constable's black eyes bulged. His face began to turn purple.

Dark sprang from the bed. He scooped up the pouch, pocketed it and stepped over the unconscious Antonio. Two strides took him close to the constable Fogg was slowly strangling. Dark lifted his arm high and cracked the constable over the head with Antonio's six-gun. Fogg dragged his arm away. The bunch of keys fell from the man's nerveless fingers with a loud jingling. He slid down the bars, slumped to the floor.

No words were spoken. Dark knelt by the inert constable and swept up the keys. By the time he was back on his feet, Fogg was waiting impatiently at his door. Dark walked out of his cell, locked that door, then quickly set Fogg free. Both men ran for the arched opening, splashing through pools of rainwater.

But even as Dark followed Fogg into the office, he knew he'd slipped up badly. Behind them, shots rang out. The constable had recovered quickly — and Dark had neglected to take his gun. The volley of shots split the night's stillness. They were intended to raise the alarm — and Dark cursed as he realized they would be heard all over the town.

Fogg was already at the front door, standing half in and half out of the office as he looked up and down a street made hazy by the pouring rain.

'The horses there?'

'Yep — but those shots have been heard up at the saloon. Someone's outside. They're not sure what's going on yet but — damn!'

He swore softly as more shots rang out.

'Now they've got it figured. They're calling to the others inside. Now he's

191

been joined by two men, three, all brandishing pistols, they're heading this way . . .'

But Dark was already moving. He'd located their hats, gunbelts, and the two long guns — rifle and shotgun. He strode to the door. As they jumped down into the dust that had been transformed by the rain into slick yellow mud, they sorted out the weapons, buckled on the gunbelts. As cries rang out accompanied by the splash of running feet and the crack of the first wild shot, Dark and Fogg leaped aboard the horses standing miserably at the hitch rail.

Then they were riding for their lives, heading up the hill towards the church, desperately flattening themselves along their racing mounts' necks to avoid the hail of bullets that began whistling over their heads.

18

The steep street curved right after fifty yards. The change in direction took Dark and Fogg out of sight of their pursuers. They were rapidly approaching the church with its open bell tower, and had pulled well away from the men chasing them on foot.

But the crackle of gunfire coming from those men had travelled far on the night air. Higher up the hill, beyond the church, figures could be seen running from houses. Lanterns were haloed dots of light swinging in the dark and the rain.

Suddenly the chasing men came round the bend behind Dark and Fogg. Again those men had clear targets, again the gunfire crackled. And now there came a reaction from the men with the lanterns. As Dark and Fogg drew level with the church a shot cracked, then another — and, with a shrill squeal, Fogg's horse went down.

Yells of triumph rang out. Fogg rolled clear of the stricken animal, paused to claw his rifle from its boot. Covered in glistening mud, he sprinted towards where Dark had drawn rein.

Dark waited, head ducked against the rain, struggling to hold his excited mount. He knew they were trapped. Men were closing in from behind and ahead. The gaps between the adobe houses were narrow and choked with litter. There was no obvious escape route, no time to think. They were outnumbered and about to be overrun.

'Make for the church,' he shouted to Fogg.

The building was surrounded by a low wall, beyond that a small garden. Dark swung down from the white horse, grabbed the Remington and ran in through the open gate. Fogg came splashing up behind him as he turned the iron ring on the heavy door and pushed it open.

Quickly they stepped inside, closed the door, threw home the bolt.

The atmosphere was cool and dry. They could smell ancient timber and incense. Light seeped in through high windows. Colourful murals were painted on the walls of a room furnished with low, heavy benches, an altar with a white cloth and ornate silver candlesticks.

'That bolt won't keep them out for long, we need those benches.'

Dark nodded, sprang to the nearest and with Fogg's help manoeuvred it so that it was up against the door. They pushed another behind it, stood back breathing hard.

'That'll hold them,' Dark said.

'There could be a back way in.'

'I'm hoping there's a back way out,' Dark said.

He ran down the aisle between the remaining benches, heard the click of Fogg's gun being cocked as the first fists began hammering on the door. But a quick reconnaissance of the church's interior told him that the small hall they were in was the only room. And there was no back door.

Back with Fogg, he told him the bad news and listened for a moment to the incessant pounding on the heavy woodwork, the roars of anger.

'It's a show. I don't think they'll break the door down, or fire on their church.'

Fogg shrugged. 'Matters not. They can camp out there for a week and starve us to death.' The word seemed to jog his memory, and he looked critically at Dark. 'What about you? You ripped that wound open. Are you still bleeding?'

'I'll live. But I don't think the *rurales* will wait for a week — and that gives me hope.'

Fogg considered what Dark might be getting at, then nodded agreement.

'You're right. So far they don't know we're Texas lawmen. Wouldn't have made a scrap of difference when they were holding us, readying the firing

196

squad, in full control — but now we're loose they might be willing to listen, be open to offers.'

'If we had something to offer,' Dark said wryly.

'*Somebody* murdered that barman,' Fogg pointed out.

Dark brightened. 'Of course. And you think it was Antonio, or King?'

'Or someone they put up to it.'

'Is that of any use? Antonio's one of them, the *rurales* are likely to stand behind him.'

'True,' Fogg said, 'but if things really begin falling apart, that tall Mex might give up King, blame him for the killing to save his own skin. And if we can prove we didn't do it — '

'Or do enough to cast doubt. If we can do that, they may be willing to let us go after him.'

There was a sudden silence as the pounding on the door abruptly ceased. In the quiet a more measured voice was heard talking. Then a jabbering of Spanish. A sharp command. More silence.

'That's the *rurales*' big chief,' Fogg said quietly. 'The fat man I met in the jail office. If he's got Antonio with him, now's a good time to let that feller know we're interested in King, not him.'

Dark nodded. 'He'll remember you. You do it.'

Fogg stepped closer to the door.

'*Hola, Capitán?*'

'*Sí?*'

'We need to talk.'

'Hah! First you two come on out, then we talk.'

'We spoke in your office. My name's Clarence Fogg. What I didn't mention is I'm Marshal of Del Rio. John Dark's my deputy. We came to Pueblo Pequeño after the man who kidnapped his wife. That man is the bank robber, Nathan King — and we believe he murdered the bartender, Mario.'

A heavy silence. Someone talking in a low voice. Then louder as it developed into an argument in rapid Spanish. Again the sharp command. Then:

'Open the door.'

'Only enough to let in one man — that's you, Capitán.'

'OK. *Go ahead, do it.*'

Fogg looked at Dark. He shrugged. Together they shifted the benches. Then Dark moved back from the door, picked up the Remington shotgun and cocked it. Fogg put his shoulder against the door, drew the bolt, released the latch and let the door open a crack.

The *rurales* captain squeezed through. As he did so a heavy weight slammed against the outside of the door, driving Fogg backwards. He recovered, slammed his boot down on the floor against the door's bottom sill then put his shoulder to the heavy timber.

Before he could close the door, Antonio had slipped through. Blood was trickling down the side of the tall Mexican's rain-washed face. His black eyes were ugly.

The door clicked shut. Fogg slid the bolt.

'We said one man,' Dark said. He

lifted the shotgun. 'Anyone else steps through that door, you two die.'

The *rurales* officer shook his head. Rainwater dripped from the peak of his cap. His uniform was soaked through.

'Is no problem. The people are dispersing, going home.' He strutted away from the door, looked from Fogg to Dark. 'If you are lawmen, where are your badges of office?'

Fogg quickly pulled his shield from his vest pocket, flashed it. Dark did the same.

The officer shrugged, as if proof of their official status was after all of no importance. He looked at Antonio and grinned. Dark thought a silent message passed between them, but their dark eyes revealed nothing.

'So tell me about this man King,' the officer said.

'He robbed the Del Rio bank, crossed the Bravo with another man,' Fogg said. 'On the way here, they kidnapped this man's wife.' He switched his gaze to Antonio. 'You said there were a dozen witnesses to the murder of Mario. I think there was just one.'

The officer grunted. Antonio opened his mouth to speak, and was silenced by the officer who shot a glance at him and gave an almost imperceptible nod.

'*Tiene razón*,' he said to Fogg. 'There was just the one witness.'

'It was the man called King.'

That was Antonio. He had moved unsteadily away from the door and was sitting slumped on one of the benches. His swarthy face was pale. He was losing blood from the head wound, and weakening. But Dark also recalled that this man had lost money at the mine. Perhaps he, too, would be glad to see the back of Nathan King.

'King is a liar,' Dark said. He eased down the shotgun's hammer, deliberately softened his voice. 'He tried to kill me five years ago. He's trying again, but this time he's gone too far. He's involving other men. Mexicans. The innocent people of Pueblo Pequeño.'

This was for the officer's benefit.

Dark let the implications sink in, let the pause lengthen, then said, 'If I can bring him in my wife will be safe, I will be safe — your people will be safe.'

'Where is he?' Fogg said quickly. 'King, and the other man, the outlaw Rick Tombs?'

'Tombs has gone, he was not welcome here,' the officer said. 'King is . . .'

He hesitated, glanced again at Antonio, and came to a decision.

'King is here now, in town, with the woman.' He jerked his head at Dark. 'Come, we will show you where he is and then you can settle your differences.'

19

But King had gone.

The gunfire that had alerted the townsfolk and the *rurales* to the jail break had also warned Nathan King. When the captain — José Díaz — led them on foot up the hill to a house on the edge of the dripping pine woods, the door was wide open, the lamp still burning on the table, but the house was empty.

'I know where to find him,' Dark said.

Antonio had stumbled down the hill from the church, making for the jail where the doctor was attending to the constable. Díaz was standing with Dark and Fogg inside the empty house listening to the drumming of the rain on the roof, the muted roar as the floodwaters tumbled down the rutted street.

'*Sí*, of course, he has fled to *la mina*,' Díaz said with conviction. 'It has a story as old as Pueblo Pequeño. I also know King's story, his partnership with Antonio, the money thrown down a hole in the ground. But that was always to be expected: *la mina* is more than a match for stupid people who dream of riches and exploitation.'

'King's thinking more of revenge,' Dark said.

Díaz shrugged, not understanding. Dark had no time to explain. He hurried on, 'Fogg needs a horse.'

'*Por supuesto*. We will go back down the hill. You will pick up your horse, we will continue to the jail. There is a stable . . . '

The walk back down the hill, the stripping of Fogg's saddle from his dead horse and covering the remaining quarter-mile to the stable behind the jail for a fresh mount for the marshal took ten minutes. From the *rurales*' office they borrowed two oil lamps, another shotgun for Fogg, shells for rifles, shotguns and pistols.

Five minutes later, with water bottles filled, they were hammering out of Pueblo Pequeño on their way to the gold mine and a showdown with Nathan King.

The rain, incessant, torrential, showed no sign of easing.

20

The unmarked trail leading up through the woods and along the base of the cliffs had been washed away. Where previously there had been hard earth covered by a carpet of dry, crackling leaves and twigs, now there was a greasy slope that tested the horses' nimble footwork and once, late in the ride, sent Dark and his white horse sliding fifty feet down the slope and into the trees.

Once again Dark's wound was ripped open. He struggled back up the slope, hanging onto the horse's tail, several times losing his footing. Back with Fogg he wiped off the yellow mud, washed his eyes and mouth with water from his canteen — and they pushed on. But the bad weather slowed them down. To cover the twenty miles between Pueblo Pequeño and the mine took almost three hours, and every minute, every yard, Dark was fretting and fuming with impatience and fear.

'Easy does it,' Fogg said once — and once was enough. Dark snapped back at him. The marshal clamped his jaw, kept the reassurance he clearly felt might help the other man firmly to himself. Dark was immediately repentant, but too busy with his own thoughts to apologize. They rode on, the silence strained.

They were as good as feeling their way along the base of the cliffs. Rain was a sullen downpour, flattening the tops of the trees, pouring from their hat brims. The swollen skies were leaden, pressing down on them, and there was never enough light at ground level for them to see more than a few yards ahead.

Navigating by guesswork, judging the distance covered in much the same way that a yachtsman calculates his dead reckoning, Dark finally drew rein.

'About here,' he said. 'Maybe fifty

yards up the slope.' He looked at Fogg. 'Now that we are here, I don't know what to do, don't know what King expects. If I knew that, I could do the opposite and take him by surprise. But maybe that's exactly what he expects me to do, and he's planning on beating that double bluff with something — '

'Cut it out,' Fogg said bluntly. 'The mine's up there, we walk in bold as brass, put a light to the lamps and go after him. Waste of time trying to outguess the man. He's got Cath. That means *whatever* you do he's got the advantage. So we probe, react when he acts.'

'Yeah, right,' Dark said. 'I'm sorry I bit your head off back there. Looks like I need you on my side.'

Approaching the mine after five years' absence gave Dark a weird feeling of déjà vu. When they'd tethered the horses under the trees, gathered guns and lanterns and walked back across the small clearing, he was amazed to see that the crude rampart he had constructed so long ago was still stoutly guarding the entrance.

They stopped hard up against the cliff face, listened, but could hear nothing for the monotonous hissing of the rain. Throwing caution to the wind they rushed forward, leaped over the rampart and dropped flat on their faces.

And did some more waiting.

Nothing happened.

They twisted their heads, in the gloom exchanged sheepish looks. Then they climbed to their feet and, safely out of the rain, lit the oil lamps and placed them on the rampart.

'Look there,' Dark said, pointing.

A trail of wet footprints led deep into the mine. Made by two people. The trail wet enough to suggest they'd passed that way recently.

'We know that anyway,' Fogg said, reading Dark's thoughts. 'King got out of Pueblo Pequeño fast when he heard the shooting. That puts him no more than half an hour ahead of us.'

Dark was sitting on the rampart.

Rain was falling on the back of his neck. The Remington shotgun was propped at his side. His hand was under his shirt, fixing the dressing that was stiff with dried blood and soaked with fresh.

'I already told you there's only one other way out of here,' he said. 'So does King know that? — or is he plunging in blind, his one idea to go so far then sit tight and wait for me to walk onto his gun?'

'I'd say he doesn't know of the other way out, but he's sure to find it if he goes in far enough.'

'Right. And then what? Take the new way — or stick with his plan?'

'It's like I said,' Fogg said. 'We probe, and react. Only King knows what he's going to do. Only thing we can do is go in after him.'

Dark climbed stiffly to his feet, picked up the Remington, grabbed an oil lamp.

'Let's do that.'

The tunnel sloped gently downwards.

After a few yards the sound of the rain had faded. A little further and it had gone completely, and all they could hear was the crunch of their feet, the rasp of their breathing. They walked in the twin circles of yellow light cast by the oil lamps. Every few yards they stopped and listened. Each time they heard nothing but the soft plink of water dripping.

Then, shockingly, a shot split the silence. The muzzle flash, somewhere ahead, was dazzling. The bullet came at them in a series of ricochets, sending needle-sharp stone splinters flying, whining off one wall then the other before hissing into silence somewhere behind them.

Dark and Fogg dropped flat. One lantern shattered. The flame smoked, died.

'Johnny!'

'Jesus,' Dark said, 'that's Cath.'

'Johnny, go back, he'll kill — '

Her voice cut off.

Dark sprang to his feet, yelled, 'Cath,

I'm coming,' and took a step forward.

Fogg's hand shot out, hooked his ankle. Dark went down heavily, cursed, tried to rise. Fogg wriggled forward, used his weight to hold him down.

'That's what he wants,' he said softly. 'Probe, react — remember? But for Christ's sake think first.'

They were still flat when two more shots cracked, two more slugs came ricocheting up the tunnel, whined into silence.

'Wait,' Fogg said.

Seconds crawled by and became minutes.

Fogg said, 'Right, I'd say he's done what he intended and gone on his way — so now we move.'

He stood up. A shot cracked. The slug ricocheted off the walls, splintering the rock. Fogg grunted, dropped onto one knee then tipped lazily onto his side.

Dark ran to him. The marshal's face was white. The front of his shirt near his right shoulder was already dark and wet with blood.

'Easy,' Dark said. 'Keep still.'

He ripped open the wet shirt, saw the ugly hole. He tore the shirt, wadded the cloth, placed it over the bloody wound.

'Put your left hand over that,' he said. 'Tight as you can. I'll finish with King then come back.'

He recovered the shattered oil lamp, lit the wick, lowered the flame then placed the lamp close to Fogg so that his body shielded it from the draught. He gave the marshal's shoulder a reassuring squeeze, then picked up the second lamp. After a moment's hesitation he abandoned the Remington, took Fogg's Winchester and started down the tunnel.

Dark had no idea how far it was to the fissure that had let him out of the old sealed tunnel and saved his life. Memory of that time was unclear. He had been losing blood from his severed fingers. Minutes, hours, had passed in a blur. His guess was that it was now no more than a hundred feet ahead of him — and even as the thought crossed his mind the light from the oil lamp washed over the pile of tumbled rocks, the vertical gash of the new opening, and Dark felt the faint breath of fresh air on his face.

King would have felt that fresh air. The man had worked the mine with Antonio. He would know the old tunnel, know that it went deep and there was no way out — and he would not risk being trapped.

With a surge of excitement Dark clambered over the rocks and entered the tunnel that had been his means of escape.

Now memory came rushing back. He was still following a down slope, but he knew that before long the ground would begin to rise. The circle of light wavered before him as the lamp swung to and fro in his hand. He held it low, aware that King would be watching for that very sign; would be doing what he could to hide the light that he undoubtedly carried.

Then the floor of the tunnel *did* begin to rise, and Dark knew that from there on he must proceed with special care. He debated: douse the flame and continue in the dark, or risk being seen?

Even as he tossed a mental coin and knew that in full darkness he would be severely handicapped, he became aware of a muted murmuring. He plodded on, listening, frowning, stumbling over the uneven ground, banging the precious lamp against the smooth rock walls — and becoming ever more perplexed as the murmur grew to dull roar that soon was blotting out the clatter of his footsteps.

Suddenly, ahead of him there was a light.

And at once, the source of the thunderous roaring became clear.

At the far end of the level section of the tunnel, King and his captive were illuminated by the yellow light of an oil lamp. They were standing facing Dark. King was holding a pistol. Cath was on her knees. King's free hand was gripping her shoulder, holding her down.

They were standing on the edge of the gully into which, five years ago, Dark had almost fallen. But it was no longer a dry wash. Waters from the heavy rains falling on the mountain's steep slopes were cascading like a waterfall through the opening beyond the gully. And unseen and from an unknown source — perhaps a yawning fault much higher up the mountain that opened into stygian subterranean passages — thousands of gallons of water were tumbling through the bowels of the earth to come boiling out into that gully in a raging white torrent that roared across the tunnel and itself disappeared into another opening, another subterranean passage plummeting down, down, down . . .

'Johnny! Go back. He'll kill you.'

Dark flattened against the wall. Held the lantern behind him, blocking the light with his body.

'She's right,' King called. 'But you know that. And you know it's going to be settled here, now — or you wouldn't have come.'

Dark said nothing. Again he contemplated dousing the lamp. And now he had caught up with King, it was possible. Now it made sense.

He turned. Looked at the wall, the lantern, knew that a single powerful swing of his arm would see it smashed, useless —

Then sudden movement, a violent flurry, a man's crude curses almost drowned by the roar of water.

Dark cast a swift glance down the passage. His arrival, the knowledge that he was in danger, had galvanized Cath. She had brushed off the restraining hand, clutched at King's clothing and was grappling with him. Her shoulder was hard against his hip, her arms locked around his waist. Dark heard her gasp, heard her sudden straining, wheezing, agonizing grunt of effort — then King was lifted off his feet. As

217

Cath thrust with all her strength, then released her grip, King toppled backwards. He crashed heavily to the ground, his head hanging over the gully's lip on the very edge of the raging torrent.

And now Cath was running.

She came straight towards Dark. He dropped the lamp, heard the glass shatter, jacked a shell into the rifle's breech and lifted the Winchester to his shoulder — but Cath was in the way. And now King had scrambled to his feet. His six-gun flashed in the lamplight. Flame spurted from the muzzle. A bullet whined over Cath's head. She heard it, began to swerve as she ran — and each swerve made it more difficult for Dark to get in a shot, to blast King with the rifle.

For an instant he opened his mouth to yell, to stop her, to tell her to drop flat. But, outlined against the distant lamplight, she was drawing ever closer, and still she was unhurt. Rifle to his shoulder, Dark silently urged her on.

Go, go, go. Go, Cath, go, keep running, don't —

She went down. He heard the crack of the shot, saw her fall, roll — and lie still. And now he couldn't see her. She had been silhouetted against the light from King's lamp. But that pool of light stretched but a few yards in front of King, failed to reach Cath's inert figure — and Dark's lamp was smashed, of no use.

But while I can see King, Dark realized, *he can't see me.*

In the darkness he smiled a grim, sad smile.

Cath was down. Shot, badly hurt, possibly dead. Suddenly there was nothing to lose. The hostage had been eliminated, King's advantage had been wiped out. And with the cocked rifle held high, Dark flattened himself against the wall and began his advance towards the bank robber.

King's lamp began to splutter.

The flame flickered. The light dimmed. It steadied — but now the circle of light had been reduced to a few feet.

Safe in the darkness, Dark felt his way along the passage until he reached Cath. He dropped to his knees. His hands found her. She was face down. He touched her throat; closed his eyes as he felt the throb of a pulse, strong and steady. He bent and whispered to her, his warm breath touching her ear; got no reply and blindly fumbled to locate the bullet wound, steeling himself for the hot stickiness of blood.

Nothing. If there was a wound, it was not on her back — yet how could that be? Gently he turned her onto her side. He stood up, stepped over her. As he did so, King fired another shot. The bullet hummed close to Dark's ear.

My eyes are reflecting the light, Dark thought. *I'm like an animal peering from the shadows. He can see me.*

Again he started forward. This time he kept his head down. King still couldn't see him clearly, but that was no handicap to the bank robber because, in that narrow tunnel, Dark was unable to dodge. King had steadied himself and was down on one knee. He was bracing his right wrist with his left forearm, firing carefully spaced shots. Each shot cracked wickedly above the roar of the flood waters. In the end, one would surely find its mark.

And the gap between them was narrowing.

Dark stopped walking. Keeping his eyes lowered he leant against the tunnel wall and lifted the rifle. As he did so, abruptly, King stopped firing. Dark heard him curse. Heard the clatter as he hurled the empty weapon down the tunnel towards Dark.

'John!'

'I hear you.'

'You know what's here?'

'Gold.'

There was a long silence.

'Together,' King said, 'we can make it work. You and me.'

'You killed my wife, King.'

'Remember five years ago in Del

Rio,' King said. 'I promised you unimaginable riches.'

'You were a liar then, you're a liar now.'

'Christ, John, it's *here*, you've *seen* it — '

'With my wife dead,' Dark said, 'nothing is of any use to me.'

'Don't you believe it.' King took a sly step forward. 'A man can buy anything, with enough gold.' Another step. 'Cath was pretty,' he said, and then he grinned wickedly, 'but, hell John, think about it, with your pockets stuffed with gold you can have all the pretty women — '

Dark shot him.

He shot him in the chest. Dead centre. A massive blow. The Winchester slug drove King backwards. He fell backwards into the raging torrent, his arms flapping, his eyes wide with shock, his mouth agape in a silent scream. And then he was gone, lost in the boiling flood.

Woodenly, his heart cold, Dark

walked to the edge of the gully. He fumbled in his pocket, pulled out the soft leather pouch and threw it after King.

Then he picked up the oil lamp and walked back down the tunnel to Cath.

She was struggling to sit up, twisting her head, looking for him.

'I must have tripped and banged my . . . head, I . . . ' She rubbed the back of her neck, looked towards the roaring waters. 'What have I missed? What happened?'

He helped her to her feet, held her in the circle of his arm.

'It doesn't matter. You're not hurt, *that's* all that matters — '

'John, where is he?'

'He tried to get away.'

'And?'

'He didn't make it. There was no way any man could get across that . . . that flood.'

'So he drowned?'

'Yes.'

For a few moments, in the dim light

of the fading oil lamp and with the incessant roaring making thinking difficult, Johnny Dark met his wife's eyes. He knew she was looking for the truth, knew that if she read it in his eyes it didn't matter, couldn't matter, because what was done was done and nothing they could do or say would change that, or their feelings.

'Good,' Cath said firmly. 'After five years it's over for you, so let's get out of here and go home to Laredo. On the way you can tell me all about it, everything that's happened — and then, at last, we can get on with our lives.'

'And raise a family,' Johnny Dark said.

'That, too,' Cath said, suddenly shy.

She stepped away, reached for his hand, and without a glance behind them they set off on the long walk that would take them back to fresh, clean night air and put behind them forever the gold mine at Pueblo Pequeño.

We do hope that you have enjoyed reading this large print book.

Did you know that all of our titles are available for purchase?

We publish a wide range of high quality large print books including:
Romances, Mysteries, Classics
General Fiction
Non Fiction and Westerns

Special interest titles available in large print are:
The Little Oxford Dictionary
Music Book, Song Book
Hymn Book, Service Book

Also available from us courtesy of Oxford University Press:
Young Readers' Dictionary
(large print edition)
Young Readers' Thesaurus
(large print edition)

For further information or a free brochure, please contact us at:
Ulverscroft Large Print Books Ltd.,
The Green, Bradgate Road, Anstey,
Leicester, LE7 7FU, England.
Tel: (00 44) **0116 236 4325**
Fax: (00 44) **0116 234 0205**

Other titles in the
Linford Western Library:

HIGH STAKES AT CASA GRANDE

T. M. Dolan

A gambler down on his luck, Latigo arrives in town bent on vengeance. His aim is to ruin Major Lonroy Crogan, the owner of the town of Casa Grande, and then to kill him. With a loaned poker stake, he soon makes enough money to threaten Crogan's empire by buying up property. However, danger lurks on the horizon and Latigo's plans seem doomed to failure. Will he be forced to flee Casa Grande as an all round loser?